ONE WAY TICKET

Sanno Keeler circa 1965

ONE WAY TICKET

A Novella of Cross-Cultural Experience in Nepal

SANNO KEELER

Friends World College Memories Project
Edited by Susie Daniel and Keith Helmuth

Published by Chapel Street Editions for
Friends World College Memories Project

Keeler, Sanno, 1947 – 1991, author
One Way Ticket: A Novella of Cross-Cultural Experience in Nepal

ISBN 978-0-9936725-4-5

Edited by Susie Daniel and Keith Helmuth
Foreword and Afterword by Keith Helmuth
"Remembering Sano Keeler" by Jim Spickard

Book design by Brendan Helmuth

Cover illustration:
  - Nepalese Trekking Permit issued to Sanno Keeler in 1968
Back cover photos:
  - Sanno Keeler with Surjit Singh and at
    RS Pura Agricultural School, September 1968

All images courtesy of Jim Spickard

For further information about
Friends World College Memories Project
contact Susie Daniel at fwi.journeys@gmail.com

Chapel Street Editions
Woodstock NB, Canada
www.chapelstreeteditions.com
chapelstreeteditions@gmail.com

Contents

Foreword: A Journey Through Culture & Compassion . .1

Glossary 7

Preface 9

One Way Ticket 11

Afterword: Cultural Exploration & the Quest
for Authentic Connection 93

Remembering Sanno Keeler 97

About Friends World College 101

About Friends World College Memories Project 105

About the Editors 109

Foreword

A Journey Through Culture and Compassion

When Sanno Keeler entered the inaugural class of Friends World College (FWC) in the fall of 1965, she embarked on a "world education" program of cross-cultural learning that led to the creation of this book. As a work of literature, *One Way Ticket* is perhaps as unique as the education program that gave rise to it.

Friends World College was created to advance cross-cultural understanding and to promote awareness of the social, economic, and environmental realities that are critical to human wellbeing and security worldwide. The program enabled students to live, study, and frequently do volunteer work in cultural regions other than their own. The fundamental pedagogy of Friends World College was "experiential learning" – learning from direct participation in the life and work of communities, institutions, and professional settings in various cultures around the world.

After completing FWC's four-year program, Sanno Keeler applied for graduate school at Indiana University. The report from her admission interview emphasized that she was far better prepared in the breadth of her cultural knowledge and understanding than typical applicants. Although her undergraduate education had been unorthodox, she was admitted without question.

Students at Friends World College were required to keep a journal in which they recorded their learning experiences. Each senior was then required to complete a project that brought a significant aspect of his or her learning into clear focus. Sanno Keeler composed *One Way Ticket* in 1969 as her senior project. While she said it was a work of fiction, not autobiography, she obviously drew on a collection of experiences with different people in various cross-cultural contexts, and blended them into this luminous story set in northern India and central Nepal.

The title of this story is also an apt metaphor for the kind of cross-cultural education that enabled Sanno Keeler to compose it. A good deal of higher education in those days was a "round trip ticket" to a culture of conformity. Sanno Keeler's education involved moving into new cultural realities and being changed by the experience in such a way that there was no going back – truly a "one way ticket" to an enlarged worldview.

Reading *One Way Ticket*, it is easy to see the level of insight, compassion, patience, and gentle humor the author had achieved in her understanding of what she calls "cross-cultural dynamics." These same characteristics are equally evident in the self-understanding of the narrator. As a proto-anthropologist and as a writer, she must have distilled this finely etched novella from a rich collection of journal entries. As one of FWC's first graduates, Sanno Keeler confirmed that the experiential pedagogy of the College was an extraordinarily effective avenue of higher education.

I first met Sanno when she returned to the Long Island campus of FWC to complete her senior project. Although I was not her faculty advisor, we had several conversations about her experiences and the kind of learning the FWC program had afforded. I remember her as a calm and thoughtful person who seemed to have a special sense of awareness, a kind of wisdom beyond her years.

Thinking of Sanno, I am reminded of an observation made by artist and cultural historian, Richard Lannoy, who was associated with the College program in East Africa and later in Europe. He said he was continually struck by the "incandescence of spirit" he found in Friends World College students. With this inspired metaphor, Richard Lannoy, captured a quality of awareness and openness to learning exemplified in Sanno, and in many other **FWC** students. Whether the College program can be credited with cultivating this quality, or whether students with this characteristic were especially attracted to the program is a good question. I suspect it was a combination of both factors, a fortunate synchronicity.

One Way Ticket has come to light as the result of the Friends World College Memories Project initiated by Susie Daniel in 2014. Susie Daniel, a student in the fourth **FWC** class, has taken on a research project that aims to survey, preserve, and document student journals from **FWC**'s early years. When I first read Sanno Keeler's manuscript, I was immediately and powerfully pulled back into the ambiance of the time and place in which the story is set. Yet, at the same time, I had a sense of the way the author had infused an aura of timelessness into the microcosm of her story. I was quite taken by the way she portrays the quest of the inquiring mind to understand the unity-in-diversity of the human world, of how she powerfully suffuses the story with the presence of landscape, and of how keenly her narrative grasps the joys, disappointments, and even tragedy that can accompany the circumstances of cross-cultural situations.

Long and complex novels have been constructed to portray this mix of elements in the panorama of the human story. Ponderous tomes of history, geography, and anthropology have been assembled to illustrate how the basic themes of culture, livelihood, and adaptation have worked out in different settings. Occasionally, a small gem of literary art comes to hand which, in microcosm, and with an economy of style, unfolds these major themes, insights, and conundrums of the human condition. *One Way Ticket* is this kind of book.

In the story of the journey, the characters come vividly into focus. Within the larger dimension of the cross-cultural theme, the subtle effects of particular lines etch people, places, and relationships into unforgettable images. These lines are often like the movements of a sidewalk artist, who can portray the essence of a face with a few quick strokes. There is an incident in *One Way Ticket* where this talent for sketching is knowingly described - a description that makes me think the author was reaching for the same art in her writing. She frequently achieved it.

One Way Ticket is a multi-level journey. In addition to memorably portraying landscapes, city streets, village settlements, and people, the author captures thoughts, feelings, perceptions, and nuances of relationship that are ordinarily illusive and often fleeting. But more than this, in a number of places she puts her finger on a certain quality of experience that eludes overt expression, but, nonetheless, will be intuitively recognized by those who have shared something like it.

There is a real freshness in the writing, but at the same time a kind of wistful and almost tragic aura. I kept thinking as I began reading, this is not what it seems, a story just about trekking to a remote village of an ancient culture. There was something a bit ominous about it from the start. My intuition proved correct. Even in those more innocent times, the problematic impact of modern Western culture on still remote traditional societies was being prefigured. At one point, the narrator reflects on the seeming "innocence" of the free-floating hippy culture that had installed itself in Kathmandu. She concludes that for her "consciousness is above innocence." With this kind of comment – and there are others like it – the story develops an undertow that heads for deep water and a dramatic twist.

Keith Helmuth
March 2015

Glossary

Words Listed in the Order of Appearance

- **kurta** – a long, collarless, shirt-like upper garment worn by men and women.

- **khadi** – hand spun, hand woven cloth; usually cotton, may be wool, hemp or silk.

- **sari** – women's drape type garment five to nine yards long and two to four feet wide.

- **terrai** – a belt of grassland, savanna, and forest at the southern edge of the Himalayan foothills.

- **sahib** – generic term for a European or American in India; originally "master" or "sir."

- **Tihar** – five-day long Hindu festival celebrated in Nepal.

- **pooja** – Hindu ritual performed to honor a deity, celebrate events, or welcome a guest.

- **roxi** – common alcohol drink in Nepal.

- **malas** – a set of beads used for counting while reciting mantras.

- **wallahs** – denotes engagement in vocational activity, i.e. a rickshaw wallah (driver).

- **jodhpurs** – full-length trousers, worn for horseback riding.

- **Maoists** – followers of Mao Tse Tung's (Mao Zedong) version of communism.

- **mund** – unit of measurement for weight in Nepal.

- **Hari Krishna** – sixteen word Vaishnava mantra originating in the *Upanishads.*

- **jaggery tea** – jaggery is a low refinement sugar that retains mineral content.

- **charpoy** – a light bed strung with rope or webbing.

- **dhai chudra** – flattened rice and yogurt breakfast.

- **kukri** – large Nepalese knife with an inward curving blade. Used like a machete.

- **paise** – Indian coin. One hundred paise equals one rupee.

- **sadhus** – India's wandering holy men.

- **darshan** – receive a "vision," an "auspicious sight," beholding a deity.

- **beedi** – a thin Indian cigarette.

- **Sikkim** – a kingdom lying to the east of Nepal.

- **Brahmin** – high caste in India; a person of this caste.

- **dhoti** – long loincloth traditionally worn in southern Asia by Hindu men.

- **tika** – forehead decoration.

- **Ganesha** – highly revered Hindu deity: god wisdom, knowledge, remover of obstacles.

- **ghee** – clarified butter.

- **thumba** – a measure of liquid volume in Nepal.

- **jherd** – alcohol drink in Nepal.

- **manas** – a measurement of rice.

Preface

One Way Ticket is my senior project for Friends World College. It is an attempt to present a study of cross-cultural dynamics in story form: what happens when a Westerner is placed in the Third World (in this case Nepal), how does she react, how does she feel, what are her thoughts.

It is not intended to be autobiographical, no more than any story reflects its author's thoughts and experiences. The characters are fictional.

Sanno Keeler
August 1969

.. I ..

I sat on a bus in northern India, a sulk tightening my lips and deepening into a frown. My braid was coming loose in the wind from the open window, and tiny strands of every color teased my nose and neck.

The bus was one of the overland companies' taking people to and from London and Delhi. It was a giant metal balloon filled with sterile air, maddeningly splattered with droplets of polite conversation. Cheap, it provided food and bedding (Spam and sleeping bags) and it got you to your destination in the incredible time of two and a half months. I joined it in Delhi on a side trip to Nepal, in a moment of weakness, thinking it might be a pleasant change from third class trains.

"Would you like a biscuit?" The voice came from across the aisle.

"No, thank you."

"Sure?'

"No thanks." They wouldn't dream of eating Indian food. Aren't I a snob?

I was the only passenger dressed in Indian clothes, a kurta and pajama. The soft woven khadi I liked; it felt cool and loose against my skin. I rested my head on my crossed arm, eyes moving swiftly with the passing scenery. I am as easily absorbed in gazing out bus windows as I am in reading a book. My thoughts moved as quickly as the landscape.

The road to Patna was typical of many Indian roads, but no less remarkable for that. One has a sense that life is lived on the road, an endless parade of purpose and wisdom, rather than a hasty transition from home to work. It had delightful traffic; herds of multi-colored goats, ox-carts full of hay or goods bound for market, small and bright horse carts stuffed with families, an occasional camel, hundreds of bicycles weaving in and out among the pedestrians and arrogantly giving way to a passing car. Horns blow constantly. Women walked with water jugs balanced on their heads, saris blown by the wind. A man squatted by the roadside, urinating. As always this was ignored, his privacy respected. I heard a few snickers from the bus. We passed water holes filled with glistening black water buffaloes, noses and ears showing above the water, and possibly a patch of rump. Once in a while one might see a white bird perched on its head, providing a pleasing contrast in black and white. Small boys played along the bank or bathed while the women washed clothes, slapping each piece against flat stones. The life of the terrai unfolded before us. The people inside the balloon quietly folded the pages of their Agatha Christies.

Everything was dusty. The fields were dusty, the trees were dusty, even the people were dusty. Still the colors were pleasing, bright and dull pastels of earth and sky and grass. My spirits rose.

The handsome blond Australian across the aisle caught my glance. He shrugged towards the outside. "Sordid, isn't it?" he said conversationally. I ignored the bait.

The first time the bus stopped it was already late in the morning. The symbionts emerged methodically, and with the usual knack groups have of sticking together despite inconvenience, piled into one teashop. They sat around complaining because the service was so slow. The driver sat down and grabbed the first cup of tea. He burned his tongue on a hasty sip and his beard shook. Looking around, he cornered me.

"You say you're studying here?"

"Yes."

"How long you been in India?"

"About nine months."

"Speak Hindi?"

"Some." Actually I spoke it quite well, but I wasn't anxious to become group translator.

"How can you stand this country?"

"I love it here."

"Love this bleeding country? You're daft! These people are the filthiest creatures I've ever come across. They are stupid. No, don't shake your head, I'd wager that if you brought in a good anthropologist who really knew what he was doing, he'd prove they were stupid."

"They are *not* filth…"

"…the only thing lower than an Indian is a hippy." He spat out the words. "If I had my way I'd let 'em starve. All the ballyhoo about population, why England has a higher density of population and look where their standard of living is. These people are lazy. Look at all that unused land we passed. Population, what? We ought to sterilize the males, keep them from multiplying. You've got the same problem in the States with niggers. You've been letting go the controls and then you wonder why there's riots. Colored people are more violent – that's a fact and I can't figure out why people are scared to admit it. In fact the country in this world I most respect is South Africa. Apartheid is the only moral solution."

The tirade continued. To me it was a theater of absurdity and it was an effort to take him seriously, for his anger was genuine. Every time I protested, I precipitated an even more emotional stream of invective. Finally I stopped him and said, "I'm not going to argue with you. But I want you to know that I disagree with every word you've said so far." I said it matter-of-factly; I was in no mood to face his wrath. The faces around me were expressionless, perhaps embarrassed that the smooth surface of their lives had had for a few moments a hint of a storm.

The driver sneered. "You're a romantic fool!" Not such a bad epitaph if one considers it carefully.

I climbed back on the bus in a sour mood. I had found in my travels that I tended to divide people in two classes, fully aware of the implication of snobbery in my analysis. The first was a rare bird, quite difficult to identify as he usually assumed the protective coloring of the species he moved in, with an adaptability that would astonish a naturalist. He was the type of person who becomes discouraged with the sights, the tourist attractions, and the constant superficial flow of events. Relationships with people take precedence over all else; it is the lives that one touches and is touched by that give depth and meaning to the experience. Understanding the culture leads such a man to a glimpse of the underlying human bond of all men, and once caught, he will always be chasing rainbows. It is not just the loneliness of the individual that strikes him, it is that he loves, sorrows, hates, and experiences joy with an intensity which is often astounding. Each man is a world; this we have in common.

The other bird is easy to identify from his bright coloring and outlandish appendages, a tourist who flits from place to place on guided tour. He is well insulated against discomfort (emotion), seeing the world through the lens on his camera. He is carefully shown only those aspects of a culture that will amuse him. He is never asked to alter his style of living at all except in those annoying moments when he must remove his shoes before entering a temple, convinced that they will be stolen before he returns. He derives enjoyment from these travels. What is amiss then? What he doesn't realize is that he may be walking all over someone. One cannot be entirely protected from a culture, nor can people be protected from him. Most of the bus travelers who I neatly fit into this stereotype, affected no one but themselves inside the bus.

It was when the bus stopped that things began to happen. They emerged from the bus mini-skirted, joking and talking loudly. The bus mascot, an enormous German shepherd, escorted them. The inevitable crowd gathered, fascinated by the strangers. Churchill hurled himself at them, barking in frenzy. The driver's wife tried to hold him back, albeit with a noticeable lack of enthusiasm, laughing unpleasantly. The edge of the crowd surged back like an ebb tide, tripping over one another, laughing. Laughing. That first day I nearly cried; people were so good-natured about it, even with the entire busload laughing at them with clever and pointed jokes. Some clapped approval; "Go to it, Churchill, chew up the bastard!" Friendly questions were cast out from that sea of faces, curious questions ignored and resented.

Once Churchill snapped at a man, ripping his dhoti. Someone whispered with a grin, "They're training him to attack Indians. Isn't he super?" I wanted to scream at them all. I left the group then, plunging into the crowd and attempting to disappear at least as much as an American can disappear in India. The stares went right through me.

It was a source of pride to me that Churchill could not trust me. He growled at me constantly. He must have been confused as to whether I was friend or enemy; I am dark for a sahib and my dress was certainly suspect. He chose the path of constant surveillance. My seat was his throne.

He spent most of his time aboard curled up where my feet should have been. At first my feet and his middle co-existed peacefully, but soon the very hint that an appendage of mine would encroach upon his territory would elicit a deep growl. If it came to a showdown, the driver's wife would intervene with a reluctance that indicated it was only convention that forced her to admit my status as a human being was superior to his. Now and then I reached down and patted him as an appeasement gesture. He endured this, but never did his tail thump encouragingly as it did for others.

* * * * *

Before long I became aware of a curious drama enacted on the Patna road. A contest was held between lorries and other vehicles. The lorries were enormous and battered in pastel colors; you'd think a goat could kick them in pieces in a trice. The road itself was a single lane of asphalt just wide enough for one lorry with wide dirt shoulders. They played "chicken," or who-gets-the-right-of-way, when they met coming opposite directions. It was a battle of wills… and nerves. Cars gave way without question in the face of the lorries, pulling out onto the dirt, although often they would similarly challenge others of their own size. I got a kick out of the fact that our driver invariably lost the contest. He cursed as he pulled over to the shoulder, but he pulled over.

Just at dusk we began to encounter a large number of lorries. Time and time again he pulled all the way over to the side of the road, choking in the dust. I could feel the tension mounting. I suppose he'd reached his limit, for the next lorry he faced stolidly, jamming on the brakes. He stood exactly half on the pavement and half off. The lorry stopped in front of him. He swore and grimaced. The lorry driver and his two passengers grinned back; one was a European - that rubbed salt into the wound. Our driver shouted, "Godammit, I won't move a bleeding centimeter!"

Now he had the rapt attention of his passengers. The others couldn't hear his words, but they saw his face and laughed at it. So they stood, one furious, the other amused. Suddenly the lorry's engine started up. The huge vehicle inched forward. There wasn't any space to spare, but he wasn't turning his wheel. The metal side of the lorry gently touched the bus. Churchill jumped at the window barking crazily. Our driver hurled insults. Such a din they certainly would hear now. I watched their faces split into wild laughter, amused by the antics. They waited proudly, confident of winning the contest. They were giving the sahib plenty of time in which to move. But our driver sat there, his profanity increasing in volume by the second. And stubborn; he could wait there the night if necessary. But that was his mistake. This was a battle of nerves, not endurance.

The lorry driver's expression changed; it said 'screw you' as plain as day. The lorry moved forward. There was a screech kof metal on metal as the side of the lorry pulled off the side window of the bus. It fell to the ground, tinkling incongruously. There was a continuous harsh scrape as the enamel chipped off the entire length of the bus. I sat convulsed in silent laughter. At most it was a tied game, and a dubious one at that.

Our driver faced his passengers as the lorry roared off into the distance with a farewell toot of his horn. "One of these days I'm going to kill one of those bastards!!" he screamed, tears of fury in his eyes. Faces watched him blankly. He stomped off the bus.

At the next rest stop the entire busload retreated to the bushes to empty its collective bladder. The driver's young wife collected rocks and pieces of brick. Not finding them noteworthy specimens, I looked at them curiously. She piled them on the floor by her seat. At dusk she opened her window and threw them at the passing lorries. I started with amazement when I first heard the CLUNK! of stone against metal; then the sound of breaking glass. I knew what it had to be, but I didn't want to believe it. I leaned forward and touched the girl ahead of me on the shoulder.

"What's that sound?"

"She's throwing stones at them." The tone was matter-of-fact, a meaningless piece of information imparted. I leaned heavily back. It's too absurd to be real. Another clunk. And another. That's it. I can't just leave it like this. I walked to the front of the bus.

"Hey," I said, "please don't continue doing this."

"Keep your stinking nose out of my wife's business!" snapped the driver, swerving the bus and crushing a chicken under the wheel.

"Yes, do," added his wife with distinct disgust. I returned to my seat.

* * * * *

The sky was tickled pink in the morning, finally bursting out into a loud guffaw as I stood on the road. My pack sat securely on my back, my thumb wiggling hopefully, and a smile played games with the corners of my eyes. Free again, fresh as dew – the first car braked and stopped a few yards ahead. Two Frenchmen in a Landrover; I opened the door.

"Kathmandu?"

"Kathmandu, oui."

·· II ··

The Frenchmen let me off in the main square. "Come and see us," they said. "Hope you find your friend." I shouldered my pack, conscious of being a stranger in a strange city. You always feel helpless, I thought, arriving somewhere and not knowing anything at all about it or where to go. Sunlight beat down on me from an amazingly blue sky. People went about their business quietly, not staring at me. I trudged off as if embarking on a wild adventure, up the street in any direction.

Svein. That was his name. It's fun to meet people you've heard a lot about; you have a mind picture shaded by the emotions of other people's words, and then a shock of contrast when you finally meet him. He was a Norwegian like Berit, interested in Zen Buddhism, she'd said. An odd pang went through me when I thought of Berit, like biting into a sour lemon. Berit had a face like a Picasso painting, half the face remarkably distinct from the other. The last time I'd seen her in Delhi one side of her face was twisted in pain, the other rigid in an attempt to endure it. I hurried, feeling that by finding Berit more quickly, I would shorten the time of her recovery.

*   *   *   *   *

"The Everest: Cheap Rates." It was a red sign, the letters barely distinguishable under the dirt. I ducked into the black hole the arrow pointed to, feeling a bit like Alice chasing the white rabbit. It was a long tunnel I was forced almost to crawl through, emerging at the other end into a cobbled courtyard. In the center stood a Chinese stone-carved lion that spat water into a cracked basin. A few women stood there with copper jugs, talking loudly.

I pushed open the screen door, blinking once more into the darkness. In the dim light I saw a counter. An obscenely beautiful boy sat behind it. He wore an electric green T-shirt, probably inherited from a guest, and his eyes matched it. His black hair hung over a high forehead. He looked up from the book he was reading and grinned.

"You want a room? Air-conditioned, golden bathrooms, only 1,000 rupees."

"No thank you." I laughed. "I'm looking for some friends of mine."

"Americans?"

"No, Norwegians."

"They come three days ago?"

"About then."

He thought a moment. "Svein-sir? He speaks Nepali?" I nodded.

"Room 24."

The hotel was clean with five flights of narrow cement stairs and one toilet for each floor. Some of the rooms were designated as dormitories; that meant there were six mattresses on the floor which cost the equivalent of ten cents a night to sleep on. Svein and Berit's room was on the top floor and had an infinitesimal balcony, looking out over the rooftops at a fantastic display of architecture. The temples were like something out of a fantasy.

I climbed the cement stairs five flights up, hearing English voices in some of the rooms, finally reaching the top. I knocked.

"Come in." Berit was kneeling on the floor, cutting cheese. "Jessie!" She gave me a long hug.

"My god, you're thin." Berit had the fragility of cut glass. Her cheeks were hollowed out, and the angles of her bones stretched the skin. "It was that bad?" It was more a statement than a question.

* * * * *

I was playing a recorder when Svein came in. Engrossed in the music and the mystery I had sensed in the city, I did not look up. Through an open window I could see the rooftops curling up below me, and I let the music flow along my mood until it ceased to be a remembered thing but had a personality and duration of its own. It completed itself and I looked up and smiled.

Svein had seated himself on the floor by my packsack, sitting loosely with his hands resting on his knees. He was so utterly relaxed it startled me. His eyes were the color of robin's eggs. I stared at him unabashed, interested. His hair curled tightly around his head, and his smile was as natural as butter. He studied me as if it were a game.

"Hi. I'm Jessie," I said, feeling immediately that the words were out of place.

"Svein," he answered. "That was lovely."

I played again, refusing to interrupt my mood yet, the thin clear notes blending with the magic I was feeling. They listened relaxed, knowing that I was playing for myself and not for their praise.

Later I stood out on the balcony, leaning on the railing and gazing at the city. I had learned that it was Tihar, the second day of the festival of lights. I watched the women below preparing wicks for the oil lamps. In a few hours the city would be alive with lights, rows of them flickering on each available windowsill, on every balcony. Svein came out and stood by me, smiled, and then stood silently watching.

"Where are you?" It was the type of question I never ask.

He smiled again. "In my village. I wish like hell I was there." He paused. "It's one of the most important festivals. I'll tell you what is happening there. Bakslimaya is preparing a banquet. She's my cook. She has worked for several days on it now; curries with meat, and special foods. A week ago she made the special sweets, some to be given as pooja, and twists of mashed rice fried in oil – like pretzels. She's made roxi too, good sweet roxi that makes you tipsy with less than a glassful. And Rukmini – she's like my daughter – she's prepared malas for me, beautiful wreaths of flowers. It is today that brothers are honored by their sisters. I promised to be there."

He stopped talking but I knew his thoughts were continuing. We stood there perhaps an hour, involved in our separate worlds, yet aware of each other's presence. He's not a person you can have, I found myself thinking. Not that anyone can have another person… it's that he is whole and not a void waiting to be filled.

"Shall we eat?" he asked quickly, as if remembering something that had completely slipped his mind. I nodded.

Walking through the streets of Kathmandu was a real pleasure; the atmosphere seemed so charged it would burst at any moment. Swarms of people, bright-eyed, prepared their night stalls of sweets, candies, shiny brass vessels, and weavings. The cobbled street wound its way between high old buildings, the dark shops harboring glittering treasures. Hand painted signs hung over some doorways. Bicycles tingled by us, swishing. Horse carts clattered their way through, pressing all bystanders to the wall. Rickshaw wallahs called to us. Then the street would open out into a square, full of activity and temples, and religious music. Men walked by in jodhpurs and a jacket that was a cross between a magician's tails and a mandarin jacket. It was the sort of dress you might expect a hobbit to wear. One could walk the streets for months and not be bored; or deliberately lose oneself for the pleasure of finding one's way again.

We ate supper at the Blue Tibetan. Roy joined us there; that explained the extra bedding in the hotel room. He was so eager and so all-American it annoyed me. Tall and handsome and with a beard that looked irrelevant, he gave the impression that he had never made a mistake. He probably hadn't.

It was a small and dark place, crowded with all manner of people; hippies from all over the world, trekkers, Peace Corps, tourists, and a few Nepalis. Most of the dishes were Chinese or Tibetan, some of them cooked with buffalo, chicken, and pork. I was amazed at the prices. An entire meal could be had for the equivalent of 20 or 30 cents. There were posters on the wall of Mao Tse Tung. One family ran the place. The waiters were small children in perpetual motion from table to table.

"It's ironic," said Roy, "that the people here making the most profit off the tourists are the communists. Most of the best restaurants are run by Maoists."

At the next table a young woman spoke angrily. "I'll be damned if I pay for this!" She poked with her fork at the chicken neck on her plate. "It hasn't even been properly cleaned. It's disgusting." Her companion merely nodded and went on with his dinner. She raised her voice, catching the attention of most of the people in the restaurant. "I ordered chicken here two days ago and it was excellent. This is shit!

I won't pay for it."

One of the Tibetan children ran and brought his father to the table. He was small in stature and had laugh wrinkles around his eyes. He flashed a smile at the girl, but she refused to be mollified.

"I wonder if he realizes how many people come here just for that smile," whispered Svein. "He's got one of the best smiles I've seen anywhere."

The girl poked her fork into the chicken. "Look. Do you call that food? It's horrid. It isn't even cleaned."

Her boyfriend spoke quickly, attempting not to sound insulting. "She's wondering if you made a mistake."

"He probably doesn't understand a word they're saying," Roy commented to me.

"Chicken good."

"The chicken is *not* good. The chicken is lousy."

"You order. My chicken good."

"It's shit. I won't pay for it."

"You eat, you pay." The man controlled his anger well, and he spoke firmly. But he was obviously displeased.

"I won't pay!"

"You pay."

"You can't make me pay for that shit. You can't!" There was a tense silence. Several people in the room shifted uncomfortably. Finally she waved her arms. "Take it away. Take it. I don't want to see it anymore!" She was screaming at him now, tears of fury in her eyes. He took the plate.

"You pay,"

"I won't!" she yelled. The man sent out one of his children and locked the door of the restaurant.

"He's sent for the police," said Roy.

"That woman makes me ashamed of having a white skin," said Svein. "She's in the wrong. She can't judge things here by her own standards. Here once you have touched food it is defiled. Only an animal can eat it. If she had sent it back before touching it, the cook would not have objected. Now it cannot be used. And those parts of the chicken are delicacies to the Tibetans."

"Can't you explain that to her?"

"She's too upset. She's out on a limb now, and she will feel it a loss of face to give in."

Within a few minutes the policeman arrived carrying a rifle. The tirade began afresh. Svein tried to explain to the girl and then to the policeman in Nepali. The policeman backed up the cook.

"You'd better pay," said Svein finally, impatiently. The girl paid and stomped out of the restaurant.

"What a selfish bitch," said Roy.

The four of us halted with astonishment as we came out into the street. The entire block looked like Midas had passed through in the short time we had eaten. Bright golden light from hundreds of thousands of oil lamps, small enough for a child to hold in the cup of his palm, flickered from windows and rooftops, gates, every available horizontal line in the city. Most lamps were made of unfired clay, some of brass. Even the poorest hut had at least a single candle in its window.

Fireworks went off: cherry bombs, huge roman candles, pinwheels, skyrockets, fountains, firecrackers. Explosions blended with the laughter of children and the hum of excited conversation in a continuous staccato. Above the city, rockets hung for a few seconds and faded like falling stars. One moment I smelled gunpowder, the next an exotic odor of flowers. Many of the boys were hung with garlands, and there were petals in the streets. Crowds of people strolled in their best clothes; tiny infants ran about with handfuls of sweets. Dogs who had been honored the day before wandered, dried flowers still wound around their throats.

"Oh, it's beautiful," whispered Berit.

"What does it mean?" I asked.

"One of the gods – I've forgotten his name – has been in the underworld, all through the long rains. Now he is on his way up to heaven and the people are lighting his way, helping him after the months of darkness." He repeated as if to himself, "Lighting God's way to heaven."

We wandered delightedly about like children on Halloween until the last drops of oil flickered and died and the empty streets rang with silence.

* * * * *

One night I was trying to sleep out on the balcony when Roy and Berit came in. I heard soft noises of people touching, rustling. A long silence, then Roy's soft-spoken voice;

"I've wanted to do that for a long time."

"You've only known me for four days." Muted, but teasing.

"That's a long time."

I began to wish profoundly that I were asleep by now, or not there at all.

"Won't Svein mind if I make love to you?"

"Of course not."

"What a beautiful person he is."

Someone once said that three people together make an awkward triangle. Here were two of the three making love, setting the other on a pedestal for allowing it to happen. When Roy tried to seduce me the next night, expertly, I didn't care what kind of euphoric wave he was riding on. It wasn't where I was at, not then.

*　*　*　*　*

An old woman crept out on the broken stones of the Monkey Temple in Patan. The square served as a market place during the day, but now, at night, it was deserted. So empty it seemed that one might have thought it never pulsated with crowds of people and loud bargaining. Some called the old woman mad. She lived there, hiding during the day, coming out at night to scavenge in the gutters and harangue imaginary foes. The temples huddled nearby in darkness, brasswork glinting dully in the starlight.

Harsh syllables bounced on the pavement. Her voice cracked and she rose to her feet, shaking her fist, a black silhouette against the sky. No one knew who she was, or how she lived, or why she stayed there; few knew of her existence. No one cared.

We flattened against a wall, perpendicular to the square. The angry words bent us into silence. "What is she saying?" I whispered, conscious of my hand within Svein's.

"She is berating the foreigners for ruining her city. 'How dare you stand and gawk at my Gods. How dare you come here in obscene skirts? You bring only noise and confusion, and you shatter the lives of my people. Leave my city before it falls to ruin!'" He translated with admiration. "She will go on like this for the whole night. Once I listened for three hours."

Suddenly there was silence in the square and we knew the old woman was listening for us. I sucked in my breath and held it. The woman peered around, straining, suspicious. A mangy dog ate orange peels in the gutter filth. She began her tirade afresh, shaking her fist at invisible evil, sounding out the stillness.

* * * * *

Berit walked quietly into the room. I was reading in a corner.

"Darling, the doctor says I can't exercise at all for the next six weeks. And mother wired; she wants me to come home. I can't go with you to your village."

Svein looked away. "Somehow I didn't expect you would. But I hoped that by seeing it you could understand how I've changed."

Berit took his head between her hands. "It's over now, isn't it? Somehow I don't mind as much as I thought I would. We can't hope to recreate something that is gone just by understanding."

It was the first time I'd heard her speak of it. She smiled at me as if to say that she didn't mind that I was there.

"It's my fault – maybe what they call reverse culture shock. I don't know. I'm bewildered here."

"Don't be guilty, it's not just you." They stopped, possibly realizing that to continue in this vein would be like tossing a ball back and forth; it was meaningless. Yet I was impressed by the respect they showed for one another, and the caring. I wanted to say it, but couldn't.

* * * * *

Sunlight erased the shadows in the cobbles as I walked towards the river. The sky was clear as glass, revealing the ragged white edges of the Himalayas, and the air was so fresh it almost hurt to breathe. Children were playing; running, yelling, begging and the shops were open. Small mounds of fruits and sweets tempted passersby. I bought a pile of guavas and went on.

I walked by the curious directions of the Frenchman; past the blood-drenched slaughtering ground near the temple, along the river path, across a narrow footbridge, pausing to consider the contentment of an immersed water buffalo, through bright green millet fields, and finally to the forest below the Monkey Temple. A troop of macaques ignored me as I paused to watch them. One infant ran to its mother in sudden fright, and an adolescent gave a threat-bark, raising his eyebrows rapidly up and down. I raised my brows in retaliation and went on my way.

The village harbored a hippie colony. Food and lodging were cheaper outside the city, and they met and talked the day through in tiny Tibetan restaurants. By European standards theirs might have been called a simple life; straw mats were the only furniture they used, sleeping bags, and a few books. They ate in restaurants; often spending less than a half a dollar a day, and a pound of hash was more than enough entertainment for a month or two. For variety they might wander around the temples in Kathmandu or cycle out to the gardens; their diet might be varied with a large clay bowl of sweet curd or a bottle of wine. Many spent hours at the USIS Library or the British Council buried in novels. Hundreds of people lived in such a way. When their visas expired or the bitter cold of winter drove them out, they migrated to the warm beaches of Goa, some lining the Ganges for a few weeks, others traveling far south to Ceylon. When their resources ran out, many could be seen in Delhi begging in Connaught Place.

The Frenchman had rented the second floor of a two-story building, small, with one room and an enormous balcony. I found the house without trouble, whitewashed, with a splendid view of the valley. They welcomed me gently, as if filled with a subtle joy in the few days they had lived there. I gave them the guavas. The coconut shell hookah was prepared, and I joined a small group sitting in a circle on the balcony. Many smiled at me; some were talking softly as the water-pipe made its way around. It gurgled pleasantly. There was no impatience here or fear, only sunlight and the wind scratching the trees.

The hash was blended with opium, giving a dreamy lazy high. The intensity was comfortable; it didn't tear at my mind. I smoked a little, feeling the lightness surging through my body right down to my toes; a delightful rush, delicious. I wanted to bounce against the sky, and I let my imagination take me there. People stretched out on the balcony or wandered off, some passing special smiles back and forth like shared secrets. I was utterly relaxed and new, a kind of innocence.

In fact, this style of life was in a sense a return to innocence. However, even though there was no intention of evil these people seemed to leave a residue of bitterness wherever they went in Asia. For them it was an idyllic life, lived with beauty and spontaneity from one moment to another. I wondered why I had never really become involved in it. There's something missing in it for me, I don't know what exactly. Perhaps I feel that consciousness is above innocence.

* * * * *

We sat in the Camp restaurant around a table in the far corner. The wall was plastered with magazine cutouts, some of them humorous. An ancient record player scratched out ancient rock. It was loud and incongruous and one of *the* places in Kathmandu. The food was terrible, but people crowded in for the conversation. World travelers plied each other with tales of adventure, or more often a simple resume of cheap places to eat and sleep. Or they swung into the room stoned, sitting down with a curious smile. Talk-hungry wanderers haunted this place, sitting the day through. Trekkers just back from Pokhara or Namche Bazaar dropped in once or twice before their visas expired, carrying with them a freshness and often saying little.

"What are you planning to do?" asked Roy casually.

"Do? That's the typical question. As if doing is synonymous with being. I don't know, Roy. I'm too occupied with living at the moment. I want to move on from Kathmandu, perhaps trek, perhaps return to college in a few months." I hesitated, thoughts churning. "Sometimes I get the feeling that the people who live the most fully are not those who become great or powerful. They don't try to get on top of life, they're just living as deeply as they can."

I nursed a lemon tea and studied faces. Berit sat moodily staring at some with a harshness that unnerved them. Conversation was non-stop; you could tune in when you wanted to. Service was slow and haphazard. When something finally arrived there was a flurry of excitement (who is it for?) and the place was so short on dishes that before you'd put the last bite in your mouth, your plate was whisked out from under you.

Berit pulled out paper and pencil and sketched quickly like a child scribbling in fury. Several faces turned to her as she labored. She gazed at the work for a long interval before turning to Svein. "This is Swamiji." Someone else grabbed it. The group claimed it as their own, exclaiming over it, delighted to find a talent among them; it justified their hanging around. Berit closed up like a turtle.

I looked at the picture. It was powerful, powerful as the man himself, and it held your attention uncomfortably. Something of the man's charisma was captured in the few harsh lines. We left soon afterwards; the picture had been pinned to the wall by popular vote.

"I can't talk about him yet, Svein," said Berit as we walked up the street. It sounded like a plea.

Two days later she flew back to Norway.

·· III ··

It was seven o'clock in the morning as Svein and I started our first day's trek from the terrai. A whirlpool of activity was behind me. One doesn't just take off for a three-week trek without one iota of equipment, without shoes, without a return air ticket to the terrai, and without thinking about it in advance. But Svein's "why not?" had had the mystical effect of resolving all of these conflicts in the space of one day.

Most of the shops were already open in the little town, touched with red in the morning sunlight. We stopped to barter for some tangerines. The single asphalt lane was on a slight uphill grade, and behind us we could see for miles into the dusty terrai. At the end of the asphalt was a salt market, about a dozen shops selling lump rocks of salt.

"Many people trek for seven days just for this salt," said Svein.

We reached the river and walked in the cool shade of its bank for about an hour. Already the porters coming down from the hills passed us, for this was a well-travelled trail, a mountain highway, and many of them begin trekking at 3 o'clock in the morning. Across the river the trail rose steeply in loose dusty shale. The sun shone directly in my face; sweat gathered in droplets on my temples. The trail was rough on the feet. I was amazed to see that many of the mountain people were barefooted.

"What are they carrying?"

"Potatoes. They're carrying them down to the market to sell. Some carry a mund and a half – that's over 130 pounds."

"Is it their own produce?"

"For some it is. Others make a contract with a shopkeeper or a landlord, bearing things down to the terrai and bringing back goods that are unobtainable in the villages. They earn about 30 rupees ($3.00) for the trip – 5 or 6 days.

The porters passed in groups of ten or so, talking and laughing. There were nearly as many women as men carrying the large triangular woven baskets. Some looked curiously at the two sahibs; many seemed not to notice us. A few smiled and questioned us.

The trail began to switchback up. For every step we took, we slid back in the loose stones. White-grey dust clung to sweaty skin. Heat pounded into my head, and the sweat tickled as it ran down to my chin or dropped off my nose. Soon my thighs were aching and my mouth was gritty.

"I know it's not lady-like to sweat, but I'm sweating so hard it's running into my eyes and smarting!" I laughed at my own discomfort. Svein gave me a handkerchief to tie around my head.

"All you need now is a feather," he said.

It was a miserable climb and I began to doubt my sanity. In fact it was hellish; up and up and up and up, my head throbbing for each step. Hours later it seemed I reached the top, climbing in the cool shadow of a rock pass.

The wind cooled my body like water, pressing my damp clothes against my body. I was filled with the pride of accomplishing a stiff climb. Far below me stretched the terrai, flat and hot. I thought: if anyone asked me why I was here at this moment, it would be difficult to answer. I seem to be always plunging into experiences that stretch me wider and wider like the plains below. Sometimes I can feel myself growing.

It was a beautiful and hellish day, a good initiation to Nepalese walking. The trail was far rougher than any I had been over before, reaching up in the hot sunlight to 8,000 feet, and then dropping just as abruptly. I was warned against sahib's knee – Europeans often take most of the weight going down steep slopes in their knees, grinding the joints together. A day of that can put you in bed for a week. "Knees bent" I growled ferociously at myself, moving my limbs like a great rag doll.

The high pleasures of the day were the moments we stopped at tea shacks, sipping the hot sweet liquid and making conversation with the cook and other porters. (Tea cost about a cent.) Children played in the dirt near our feet and it was good just to sit awhile, resting and watching. Our presence provided at least an innovation in their lives, and I was warmed through by the smiles.

In late afternoon we reached a footbridge at a river gorge. Svein purchased sugarcane that he peeled with a pocketknife. We bit off great juicy hunks of the crisp stalk, sucking and chewing the sweetness, then spitting out the remainder. Soon there was a small mountain growing in front of us. To me it was ambrosia; I had never tasted anything so good in all of my life.

At dusk we crossed the river again, stopping at a "restaurant." It was a small home, of course, but they served rice and allowed us to place our sleeping bags on the porch. The father played with his youngest child in the doorway, clapping his hands together to the chant of Hari Krishna. The mountains loomed high and dark and the breeze grew chilly. Dark forms still passed, plodding along. I was glad when they called us in for supper. We sat eating with our fingers, rice and vegetables and the luxury of an egg. Svein's hair was like bronze in the candlelight.

Talking quietly in our sleeping bags, we heard figures rustling by like careless ghosts. Svein began talking about Nepal.

"I came here arrogantly, thinking to help these people, without a thought for whether they needed or wanted my help. Now, with what some might call romanticism, I like to think that I am confronting human problems that are common to all of us. I am a man working among men, and if I happen to have a skill that the people here want to make use of, why then I am more fortunate than they are; to me it is a great happiness to be needed. I've learned much more than I've taught, and I've gained much more than I've given, but that seems to be the way of the world."

In the morning I awoke with the faint tracings of dawn in the sky. The frozen air hurt as I drew it deep into my lungs, and I felt cleansed. I climbed out of the sleeping bag quickly so as to not be tempted to stay in its warmth, and then looked over at Svein. He was awake, his curly hair in a frantic mess, grinning.

"Good morning," I said, smiling at him.

"Mornin!"

We started immediately, not even waiting for jaggery tea. We wanted to finish with the worst part of the climb before the sun hit us. My shoulders were sore from the pack, and my thigh muscles felt like hard, painful walnuts behind my knees. But my knees are all right, I thought, thank god. We followed the river in the damp air, and as we came closer the mountain in front of us grew steeper.

"This is just one step away from being a cliff," I said as we started up the embankment. I slid back in the sand, clawing for a foothold. Farther up, steep rocks provided a kind of stair. My legs felt weak with the load on my back, and already sweat had begin to trickle down my forehead. It was reminiscent of the rough spots of the day before. What in hell am I doing? I asked myself ruefully. I stopped and tied the handkerchief around my head.

Porters passed me going down with their curious light steps. I stepped aside, wondering what the occasional comments that were addressed to me meant. I smiled or said something in English in reply. Usually they wanted to know where you were going and where you had come from, Svein had said. Sometimes I would point and say, "Okhaldhunga." It sounded like a make-believe name, but by now it was curiously fitting, for I felt as if the village were at the end of the world.

The shale was darker now, but it was just as loose and difficult for walking. The trail continued up and up, one switchback after another. I plodded on, resting every few steps like the porters. An hour and a half later I reached the first resting point. The sun had just hit the mountain, and the large clearing was filled with people, their burdens resting high on the rocks at the side of the trail. There were a couple of vendors there selling tangerines and sugar cane. I spotted Svein in the midst of the people, sitting on a flat rock. The gorge dropped so sharply I could hardly believe I had just come up it.

"You're over the worst part now."

"In America that would be at least a half day's climb. What time is it now?"

"A quarter to seven." He grinned. "Look what I've got."

It was a large luscious pineapple. We breakfasted, saying little. It was relaxing to sit in the warm sun after a vigorous climb. I've come far enough now to know I'm going to make it, I thought.

I sat watching the porters sitting, pausing, walking on. One could distinguish various types of porters. There were the men who portered for a living, carrying unbelievable loads. Their wives often wove pooja blossoms into their baskets, and one saw them in small groups at the side of the trail around dusk, cooking their rice over small fires. They seemed to enjoy each other's company, talking and joking far into the night, even though they would arise before dawn to begin the long day. Husbands and wives, and sometimes daughters, portered the family's produce down to the markets on the terrai. Women walked together, gossiping. Now and then one would see a group of Tibetans, always by themselves. Or a rich man would pass, four or five porters running ahead of him. Usually he would have a radio in hand, and for several minutes the lively Indian film music would fill the air until once again only the crunch of boot on rock could be heard. And women in bright saris, sweating and puffing, would look a trifle disdainfully at Svein and me, knowing full well we could afford porters. Twice I saw someone pass, rich and old, or rich and lame, carried on a porter's back. One would hardly suppose it possible.

"Did you know that probably less than half of the people who pass realize you're a woman?" asked Svein.

"What?" I replied, a bit indignantly.

"Some of them discuss it and they usually end up deciding you're a boté, a Tibetan man. After all you have long hair in a braid down your back and you are wearing blue jeans that obviously are not new. And the thought of a woman wearing a man's clothing has probably never occurred to them."

The morning stretched out into heat and aches, people passing, steps up and up and up, on and on. My forehead throbbed; not with pain, it simply throbbed away. I felt an emptiness in the pit of my stomach as if there were a hole there. A sharp wave of pain swept through me, leaving my knees trembling. Menstrual cramps. Shit... Embarrassed, I told Svein.

"Not the most convenient time, is it?" was his only comment. As we got ready to go, he strapped my pack onto his frame.

"You can't do that!"

"Sure I can."

That evening we reached a tiny village at the top of the ridge. The air was light and cold and a fog was settling in. It was startlingly clean; most of the buildings were whitewashed. The narrow street was paved with flat stones, too narrow for carts since this part of the world has never known wheels at all. We came upon the village out of a forest, passing first the temple and the small market square. There was a population of Tibetans here, and it was to this part of the village that Svein wove his way. The keenness of the air brought an eagerness to my feet, and the village was lovely in the subdued light.

A Tibetan family came out to greet Svein with warm smiles. "The mountain telegraph!" he said aside to me. I sank gladly down on the bench in front of the house and happily nursed a steaming glass of jaggery tea. Svein had carried a liter bottle of soy sauce from Kathmandu for them, and sat talking in the open kitchen. "You'll get a better meal here than in any other place in eastern Nepal," he said.

I watched the women moving about, preparing supper. They moved gently in their woven garments, and I wondered if I ever had seen lovelier faces. Two children played near me - a boy and a younger girl. I gave them biscuits from my pack. They stood looking at me a few moments and then resumed their play, the older child remarkably careful of the younger. It seemed to me even more strongly than I had felt at the refuge settlements that here were people living profoundly. There was a quality of living I found it difficult to capture even in thought. It was a wonder just to be watching these people.

My thoughts moved on, thinking of all that had led me to this place. The art of living lies in choice, I thought, the roads we take, the decisions we make. A myriad of choices led me here, and I know they were *my* choices, for at this moment I know I would rather be here than anywhere else. How many times I've felt my decisions were not my own; that they came from someone outside me, or just from the fact that it was the kind of decision one is expected to make. Yet the few times I've chosen inwardly, I've chosen best. To trust myself more, that is what I need to develop.

Night fell down like a blanket. Svein and I were led into a dark and bare inner room. It was our first meal of the day, and I was ravenous. After the meal we were led to a tiny room on the upper story with whitewashed walls. There were two intricately woven carpets on the cow-dung floor, startling in their brilliant colors. We slept immediately.

Early in the morning I stood alone, facing the Himalayas. They were too real to be there, frighteningly close. The sharp peaks were blood red, and a mist hid their stomachs, displaying them as immense gods. The immensity pressed on me, yet also gave me a curious sense of release, for they seemed to slash at the very foundations of our everyday existence, cutting away time and space. They filled me – was it fear? – yet demanded a great silence. Suddenly I realized why laughter seemed such an integral part of the life here, among the porters and in the villages; it was the yin and the yang, the joy within the starkness, the sweet aftertaste of a bitter lemon.

Again, I was flooded with thoughts: at times I am so powerful it is frightening to conceive of it, other times I am so little I can hardly see myself. Looking at the mountains I feel both so strongly; in the universe I am no more than a few molecules, but, standing here on a ridge, I am god-like. Nothing would exist if I did not see it. I myself am as great as what I see or as non-existent as the things I don't see.

The trail would be along the ridge for two full days, a ridge extending twenty or thirty miles at the height of 9,000 feet. The trail itself was wide and grassy; the shale had disappeared. The Himalayas floated above us, giving us a sense of suspension on some high remote point in the world, and I found myself hurrying along without effort or feeling of speed. Odd patches of mist clinging to dips and valleys completed the feeling of unreality, and the air was as cool and refreshing as a waterfall. Long green grass lent a softness to the sharp drops straight down into the river gorges, and sheep lay about like marshmallows.

I was more alive that day than I had been for several months. It was as if a burden of used-up thoughts had dropped from me, and the past was no longer pulling. The present moments were so vivid that even future and destination were gone, no thought of time or relevance. Time was the pause to feel the spray of a waterfall, the resting of one's burden on a rock.

The people were happier higher up. The path was without stones and perhaps it was easier on their feet. They passed with that odd step that eases the load – knees perpetually bent with most of the weight centered near the toes - almost on tiptoe, graceful. Some old people have travelled in this manner so long, their legs will no longer straighten and there are definite grooves in their foreheads where the headstrap has pressed. Young girls begin portering, laughing, carrying their loads with straight backs and gossiping long into the night. But in only a few years their backs bend forward, feet deformed by many untreated infections into one hard flat callous. Scar tissue is strong.

In the evenings along the trail one sees their fires and their fellowship. That night we slept with them, wrapped in our sleeping bags, feeling safer and warmer than ever before in memory. And when we woke we found the ashes of the fire were already cold, and we were alone.

Late the next morning we rested by the side of the trail. Svein stood a short distance off, looking down into the valley, his hands in his back pockets, and his feet wide apart. I think I'm a little in love with you, Svein. I like the way you talk with the people, the way you stand when you're waiting for me to catch up, the way your hand goes when you run it through your hair. I like how relaxed you are. I'm a fool.

Soon I felt an energy that seemed to come from outside myself. I hurtled along the path madly as if chased by demons, yet quite aware of every detail I passed, waterfalls, moss-covered rocks, each individual face, the trail itself as it changed over the hours. I scrambled up narrow cliffs, never losing my pace, fueled by the warmth of my body. I walked for hours without stopping, possessed by rhythm, passing through swamps of bearded trees, down cliffs and through gulleys. Finally I stopped on a rock promontory, waiting for Svein. My skin felt electric.

"You caught your second wind," said Svein when he came.

"It's great."

"At this rate we'll reach Okhaldhunga tomorrow."

We walked on as dusk approached, trying to reach a village at the foot of a dip in the ridge. Already, by the side of the path porters were gathering around fires, their heavy baskets lining the bank. Smoke wafted into our faces. We were tempted to stop, but here we could not buy rice nor have a sheltered place to sleep.

We arrived at the village when it was too dark to see well, crawling down a rock cliff to reach it. It was a cluster of thin wooden huts with no stone work in the two short streets. Svein soon found a hut that would sell us rice and provide us a place to sleep. It was a two-room hut that also served as a shop; it carried soap, rice, tea, candles, and raw sugar. A wooden platform was cleared of potatoes to make space for us. A woman built a fire with cow dung in the corner of the room and began cooking the rice. Dim yellow shadows moved about the room. A candle was placed on a shelf, flickering in the strong draft. Svein and I sat. I was incredibly weary, unable to stir. It grew colder and the night wind blew straight through the hut, creaking and groaning. I was grateful for the shelter.

A young boy handed me a charpoy and began to prepare his own sleeping place under the shelves, a narrow space on a mat. He had one blanket. Svein talked to the father of the household, both of them sitting on their heels in the position one sees all over Asia. I noticed what a good way Svein had with people; he raised them to his own level or himself to theirs. And he was light – not superficial but not over serious either. He made people want to smile.

We were served mounds of steaming rice on cold metal plates. A glass of curd sat beside each plate. "This is excellent curd," said Svein. He mixed it into the rice with his fingers. I did the same. It tasted delicious. I was ravenous, almost too impatient to chew. The curd was cold and slippery in my fingers and had a sharp flavor. Suddenly I was no longer hungry, just terribly tired.

I began to wash my hand into the dish as I had done many times in Indian restaurants. The boy stopped me, gesturing at the door and a can of water near it. "If you wash your hands into the food here, even an animal can't eat it," explained Svein. I went outside to the street. The wind was bitter.

The woman set straw mats up against the door opening, tying them to the rafters. The family vanished into the second room, and soon the candle was extinguished. Svein and I moved closer together for warmth. This could be the loneliest place I've ever been, I thought, but I feel utterly safe. The wind whined, insinuating its presence, but we were warm in our sleeping bags and full with a good meal. What more could be contentment? I lay in an odd mood – too tired to think, too happy to sleep, and aware of Svein beside me.

Morning came too soon, the black night fading into gray clouds. The woman moved into the room to light the fire. I lay stiffly, watching on my elbows and hoarding the last minutes of warmth before emerging from my cocoon. We breakfasted on dhai chudra, dried rice rolled like oats and difficult to chew.

"There have been two murders here since September," said Svein. "I didn't want to tell you last night."

"Really? How did they happen?"

"I'm not certain. They've been explained to me as drunken brawls, but I think there's more to it. This village has such an odd feeling to it."

"And I felt so safe last night!"

"You were, perhaps. This is the only hut where I feel comfortable. In these situations one begins to rely on one's feelings – so often they've proved right. You know, it's strange, but I find I make decisions here from intuition.

There's no set norm or procedure, things are changing so fast and one can't even go by one set of values. Maybe it's more human, and the mistakes are more my own somehow,"

There was a tension between us that morning. I didn't know what it was, a chasm opened as we neared the village. Instantly I was filled with self-doubts, and then dismissed them knowing well how transient are human emotions. I let it be.

Svein asked me curtly, "Do you want to stay with me in the village?" I knew this was a decision he had struggled with and couldn't make for himself.

"Oh, Svein, you know I can't," I said, answering before my feeling caught up with me. I went on as if sinking in water, "It wouldn't be right in the village. I don't care so much about myself, but I don't want to damage the respect the others have built up.

"I guess I didn't think of that. I only wished..." he stopped.

"What?"

"It doesn't matter."

At one of our many rests that day, I leaned against a tree and thought about him. Oh Jesus, I want you inside here so much it hurts. I never wanted to have a person to possess. I don't want to have you. I just want recognition, I want your touch. Tell me that to you I exist, let me be whole and real. Lord, why did I ever get into this? It's all wrong, I know it. You've just broken up with Berit. I've never wanted anyone this way. And I think you know it. Shit. There's no sense to it, I don't want to be hurting. I want to laugh, but I'm all tied up inside and it can't be forced out. I hate you.

Sometimes the world seems too full; the wind is stronger than I can stand, the sea too deep, the sun too shiny for me to bear. Sometimes I wish I were just a tree with deep roots in the earth, or a bird that could just glide on the wind and not beat her wings at all.

I was tired that last day, walked out, too tired to be miserable. Svein talked cheerfully about the village, possibly trying to brighten my mood.

"You'll be staying with Judy." He made a face, with a sidelong glance at me. "So you'll get to know her. She's got the nicest place. But I think you'll like Ernie best of all. He's not the kind of fellow you'd expect to be an anthropologist. He's not one yet, but he's gathering material for his doctoral thesis. He looks more like a truck driver, and his clothes never seem to fit him. He's one of the most genuine people I've met. He drinks a lot but never plays games with people. Sometimes I feel like a chameleon – I adapt to the people I'm with. Do you ever feel that way? In the village I'm a different person, I feel almost Nepali. But Ernie doesn't change. He isn't detached, though, he's really involved with people on a basic level. Maybe he is a little more human than the rest of us. And he's got an amazing temper."

I half listened, plodding along the remaining fifteen miles to the village.

·· IV ··

Sarah walked in from the fields, clothes as tattered as those of the woman who was teaching her to weave. She was wearing a half sari and the curious velvet blouse tied near the shoulder that most women in eastern Nepal wear. The tiny valley was like startlingly clear water at that hour, the sky bare of mist and the mountains sharp as pins. You might have thought you were walking into a fable if you had just stepped down from the ridge above, as Svein and I had, emerging from a thick green forest. Sarah looked weary. Setting up a loom was a task of Sisyphus I learned; in the night the wind would play havoc with the threads. Sarah was the kind of woman who rarely finished a project she started. She'd engaged the woman to teach her the mountain method of weaving only a couple of weeks before she would leave this valley. One could imagine her in New York, frantically trying to assemble the loom two hours before the display.

"Sarah!"

"Where have you been?' She quickened her steps. "We have been without money for nearly three weeks. Why didn't you come back when you said you would?" She looked at Svein and I could see she was trying to be angry and not quite succeeding. "You really hurt Bakslimaya, not coming for Tihar." She shook her head seriously, "She swore up to the last moment you would come for Tihar."

"I had to get a new permit and the offices were closed all through Tihar."

"Well I don't envy you going up there. Be good to her, Svein. You really hurt her. You did bring the money, didn't you?"

"Yes."

"Ernie's going to kill you. He's been saying that for days now. You better go up and see him." She turned to me. "Sorry for ignoring you, this seemed so immediate. You're certainly welcome here."

"Thanks."

Svein called up the stairs. In a few moments we heard heavy boots on the narrow wooden ladder. "You fucking bastard, I'm going to kill you. Where in God's name have you been all this time?" Svein began to explain, but he cut him short. "If you hadn't come today, I was ready to begin trekking to Kathmandu with a kukri, and if I met you, I swear I would have killed you. We owe money to everyone in the goddam square. We've been eating rice for a month, just rice, no vegetables or fruit or meat. Jesus. If we get scurvy I'll sue you. You know how much money we have left?

Twenty paise, twenty fucking paise. We've been buying on credit and you know how far that goes in this country. People are getting angry. Damn you, Svein, I was ready to kill you." He glanced at me. "Sorry about this, but I've got to be mad at this bastard."

I examined the man sitting at the top of the ladder glaring down, and I liked him. He was stocky with a heavy black beard, lively with anger. He reminded me of a pirate.

"Do you have an alibi?"

"Ja. I couldn't have it back any earlier than this." Svein was smiling; he couldn't hold it back.

"Well, now that you're here there's not much use in being mad. I ought to be wringing your neck." Ernie was suppressing a smile. "Oh hell, I'll admit I'm glad you're back. But I'll be damned if I say you're welcome. Come on up."

"Bakslimaya was ready to cut your throat the day after Tihar," he said as we climbed the ladder. "You're going to have fun ironing that out. Don't expect a sunny welcome up there either."

The upstairs room was large, the roof supported by posts. It was sparsely furnished; one bookshelf full of medical textbooks, a couple of trunks, lanterns, two small Tibetan rugs, and a wooden bed in the corner. The floor was spread with hardened cow dung.

"Ever see a floor made of shit?" Ernie asks me. "They'll never believe us when we say we slept on cow shit."

They offered me a bath. No one could have given me a more valuable gift at that moment. I creaked my way down the ladder to the corner they pointed out.

I poured a vessel of cold water over my back. I gasped in sudden pleasure; a thousand cool fingers stroked my skin, drawing out the weariness and ache. I shivered in sheer wonder, and poured again, pleasure running up and down my skin like a network of electric shocks and reaching into my very bones, down to my toes. I laughed, splashing the water, throwing it at my body as if I were a magician dispersing it to roll down in enormous drops. Soap transformed the game into a slippery delight, like being inside an ocean wave in slow motion, surrounded in bubbles and battered gently in odd currents. I finished my bath newborn like Venus cast up from the sea, leaving behind a pile of suds.

I leaned against a post, the drone of conversation outside me. I was clean, luxuriously clean and dressed in a Punjabi outfit borrowed from Sarah. Ernie handed me a brass finger bowl of roxi, a strong drink distilled from millet. It tastes like sugared gin, I thought. I'll be drunk in two seconds flat. I'm famished. Before I had sipped a third of the liquid my head was swooping and my knees felt suspiciously weak. The room was slipping and I had ceased to be aware of anything at all except hunger.

I found myself sitting in another house with only the dimmest notion of how I had gotten there. Judy, that was it, it was Judy's house. My knees hurt but I was too tired to shift them, and my head was still light as a balloon from the liquor. Svein was there, subdued and silent.

"How was Bakslimaya?"

"She welcomed me, Rukmini too, but there's a real strain.

Underneath I think she's sulking. I don't know; I can't seem to get through to her. I guess all I can do is sit it through."

Conversation floated around me, not penetrating. Judy was there, plump and blond-haired, her heavy gold earrings glinting in the candlelight. She reminded me of a Viking, long-skirted and robust. Ernie and Sarah sat talking animatedly, gossiping about the people they were working with. Svein sat cross-legged, fiddling with his pipe. Now and then I caught a comment cast to me: "Wiped out... first time I came... couldn't believe it... lucky you didn't get sahib's knees... nurse... months ago... bed two weeks."

Food came and was served agonizingly slowly. It was a vegetable curry with a tiny bit of meat, a great delicacy in the village. At last I dug my fingers into the food. I burnt my fingers in the hot rice eating greedily, but I savored the texture, heat, and flavor of each bite. Had I ever eaten? I had long since forgotten the pains in my belly and now became aware of the emptiness there. I took a keen pleasure in filling the hole; even swallowing was a delight.

After the meal Judy filled a pipe with hash and passed it around.

"Where did you get this?" asked Ernie, taking a long drag.

"The sadhus bring me some when they come up. It's darshan."

"Fantastic."

I was upside down in a roller coaster, my head turning over and over from the potpourri of roxi, hash and physical exhaustion. The room spun neatly, and I looked at faces and words through a kaleidoscope. Oh my lord. It was too much for me. My head fell onto the rug as if detached from my body. I'm glad I'm with good people, I thought, and passed out.

* * * * *

I awoke in utter darkness. Panic held me a few moments: where in all hades was I, had I gone blind somehow? Sluggish memory! I gripped myself and took inventory, at last persuading myself that if I were indeed thinking rationally it would be day out in the world. I stared until I could see a faint sliver of light and groped my way to it. A bright world hit me smack in the face as I shoved open the shutters, and I stood a while confounded.

Judy's cook smiled from the courtyard, and just as I finished dressing – or rather re-dressing – came up with two glasses of hot tea. She routed Judy out of bed and we sat on the rugs talking.

"It's crazy," said Judy as Sita left the second time, grinning impishly. The cook had left us two steaming plates of rice with vegetable curry and curds. A real breakfast! "She cheats me, complains, robs me even – I bet even now she has the better part of the curry downstairs and is eating it with her daughters. I gave her so many gifts at Tihar, new clothes for all her children, and not once did I hear a word of appreciation or gratitude. The more I give her, the more she expects. But I can't help liking her. I couldn't have survived here without her. She knows it. She's a scoundrel, but I like her."

I accompanied Judy to the school that first day, sitting in the classroom and helping with the English lesson. I came to spend parts of many days playing there. Long hours I sat in the kitchen with Sita. She was an artist at non-verbal communication, I found, and a pleasant teacher. I wandered through the village and the hills around. Okhaldhungha was a pied piper of my fantasy, and my feet never rebelled against the long walks and pauses as its wonders were revealed to my slow eyes.

The village was astoundingly beautiful, the air crisp like lettuce leaves. For me it had a magical quality; I could hardly believe that such a place could exist in reality. The stone-flagged streets, the shops and goats, temples, the costumed people; all these were escaped from some fairy tale of my youth, coming here to mock me for growing up, for letting them slip away into some hidden corner, shabby and disgraced.

* * * * *

Bakslimaya moved about the kitchen. She had welcomed me delightedly and had set a stool for me in the corner. A light steady rain of conversation accompanied the sound of meal preparation. She was attempting to teach me Nepali, and in her exuberance was telling me every word she could find which had a living example in the room. Her age was undoubtedly thirty or more (deep lines betrayed her), but the tennis shoes she wore epitomized her vitality. She bounced from one spot in the room to another with an incongruous grace. She wasn't pretty, but she was unmistakably alive and full of humor; she could make you laugh at her jokes without speaking a word of your language.

"Come in here a moment."

I walked into the other room, scattering the pigeons on the floor in fright. It was a cluttered room, all manner of debris on the floor: books, unanswered letters, school papers, dirty clothes and bedrolls. A small balcony afforded a magnificent view of the Himalayas and the village itself, for the house stood high above on the outskirts. Svein handed me a letter.

> *Dearest Svein,*
>
> *This will be my last correspondence with you for some time as I am now devoting full time to spiritual endeavor. I have as my teacher and guru Swamiji, and under his wise guidance I am at last finding that which I have been searching and yearning for. But I must sever temporarily all ties with the world, for they are holding me back from attaining the highest realms of meditation.*
>
> *You can help in two ways:*
>
> *Do not attempt to communicate with me in any way until I have reached my goal. I will then contact you if I am so guided.*
>
> *Contribute money to Swamiji, for I am now fully devoted to him.*

*I hope this letter finds you in good health. I wish you
joy in the good work you are doing.*

*Love,
Berit.*

I handed the letter back to him. Swamiji. Good Lord, how some people could get control over a person! Charisma, that was it, and Berit thought she'd found her answer to life. Poor Berit. I wonder how much of herself she lost.

"Swamij wrote this," I said. "The man she drew in the restaurant."

"Who is he?"

All of a sudden I didn't want to talk about it. How could Svein understand that kind of pain?

"A guru she followed. A bad guy." If Ama hadn't understood... I spoke again, harshly. "The woman I lived with in Benares sent me to find her. As I walked into the ashram – this is going to be hard to believe – but the moment I walked in I heard Berit screaming, not loudly, just crying as if she was hurt. I opened a door and I saw two young men beating her with ropes. It seemed that she had had a disagreement with Swamiji and had threatened to leave. I don't know what I would have done then, but when they saw me they stopped. I went over and hugged Berit. She burst into tears and asked to be taken away. She was half dead from hepatitis, Svein."

There was a heavy silence. "Ja," he said, "I know that."

"I'm sorry, Svein, I can't really talk about it. I guess it's she who should be telling you, not me." He nodded.

Bakslimaya appeared at the door and carried in the plates. She watched us as we ate, smiling, but would not eat with us. I noticed that she flirted with Svein, subtly, bestowing needless attentions on him. It was an art; she was never obvious or indecorous, yet she pleased him without his being aware of it. I could begin to understand how a young Indian wife could retain her husband's devotion without ever showing outward affection in the presence of others – in an environment where privacy is impossible.

Svein fit here, smoking a beedi and sitting hours in the dark warm corner. It resembled a marriage; he was waited upon and made much of and he enjoyed it immensely. He had no need to run to the other sahibs for emotional support; everything he needed was at home. In his way he loved Bakslimaya, and she made sure he kept on loving her. If the hours grew long he would teach Rukmini, his 'daughter', or play games in the larger room. Often he told me, he would go and smoke beedis in the square with the other men, or drink roxi at someone's home, squatting in Nepali fashion and talking agriculture or politics.

* * * * *

Judy and I sat chewing roasted lentils on a lazy afternoon. "It has been a fabulous experience for me here in many ways," she said. "The women here have been pleased to have me; in the past all of the sahibs have been men. I get along with the people wonderfully. I really do. But sometimes

I feel unspeakably lonely. I get sick of the other sahibs. I want somebody to communicate these things to, someone who can listen, someone who knows my language and cares. Ernie, Sarah and Svein – I know them better than I've known anyone, I know them all too well if you know what I mean. We're all so aware of each other's hang-ups, we seem to reach a level we can't get beyond. We know what to avoid. Maybe that's part of the problem, we stop having meaningful confrontations.

" A lot of it is sexual. I want a good screw. A year is a long time to go without any sex at all; it's hard for me. I get back to Kathmandu and I fall into bed at the first opportunity. Don't laugh; I shock myself sometimes.

"I don't want to sleep with any Nepali men. In the first place none of them attract me here, and secondly it would ruin the work I am trying to do here. Everybody knows everything that happens in this village; even a closed door is no protection."

* * * * *

It was a fresh morning. The trail was grass-covered and full of laughing children. Many of the women were clad in bright red saris, throngs of them, a sure indication of a festival. They carried pooja with them in bundles. This was to be a Hindu ceremony, but as with most festivities in the village people of all tribes would come. Animated conversation ran back and forth between Judy and the women we passed. There was excitement everywhere and the children had a half-day free from school.

"Judy-sister. Good morning."

"Good morning."

"Jessie-sister?" shyly. Already the whole village knew my name.

"Good morning."

The trail wove absentmindedly upwards, passing sheep and goats in isolated huts. The mountains showed uncertainly, white peaks dissolving into clouds, lending a contrasting reality to the mountain on which we stood. The altar stood high on a bare hillock. One could see all the way to Sikkim. There was a small canopy made of poles and brightly striped cloth, a crowd of people under it. Threaded tangerines hung above the clay temple and the whole area was strewn with flowers. The heavy scent of crushed flowers and incense blended, carried by the breezes.

Judy was greeted by many voices and she bent to hug several of the women. The priest poured spiced curd into the palm of my right hand, and I touched it to my forehead in the traditional manner. I found it tasted bitter. Immediately, we were hung with beautiful malas. I breathed deeply; there were orange blossoms on mine. Looking around, I saw that we were the only women there with malas around our necks. Each and every man including the tiniest child was decked in flowers. But when we sat down with the women I knew we had done the right thing in keeping them on, for they were enormously pleased, fingering them and smiling.

The women sat under a canopy, making malas and leaf baskets for pooja – tangerines, sweets, and pounded rice. I began making the garlands, gathering petals and catching them together with a tricky noose tied with one hand. They laughed at my awkwardness but encouraged me to continue, working deftly as they talked.

The Brahmin priest sat on the altar and began speaking. Most of the people did not listen for he was telling an oft-repeated tale, but Judy listened with intense concentration. He sat cross-legged in a white dhoti, forehead lined with three white bars and a tika of yellow. Suddenly the euphoria I was feeling so intensely bubbled over and I was left with an odd emptiness. The sun was too brilliant, the people too beautiful. On an impulse I walked away from the crowd. The moment I was out of sight, I ran down the mountainside, the wind blowing back my hair and humming around my arms. The grass was springy under my feet and I whirled around in a carefree joy.

I walked up the narrow planks to Svein's kitchen, breathing hard from my run. I listened to my footsteps on the dusty wood.

"Svein!"

"Come in."

The door creaked as I pushed it and a chicken clucked and clambered out of my way. Svein was sitting at his desk, his hair uncombed, papers scattered.

"It was beautiful up there, but after a while I just couldn't take it." Blood warmed my cheeks. Svein came to me and kissed me, hard. We held each other a few moments, I with a queer knot of joy inside me. I felt like crying but smiled instead as if I might break like a tight balloon.

I heard Svein laugh lightly. "I wasn't going to do that."

"I know."

We both heard loud movements in the kitchen. The door was open. I don't think I left it open, I thought. Moments later Bakslimaya appeared at the door and beckoned to Svein. He left without a glance at me, and I heard a murmur of voices from the next room. The room seemed larger and emptier, and the clutter was worse than usual. The pigeons pecked at rice on the windowsill. I watched them.

"You'd better go now." The words were quickly said but the seconds following them seemed long. His fingers touched my hair. "I'm sorry." He didn't seem able to say more.

"It doesn't matter, Svein."

* * * * *

We were alone in Judy's room, the others having gone out to buy roxi. The kerosene lamp lit up Svein's face grotesquely. He moved closer to me.

"How are you doing?" I asked. It was almost a whisper.

"It's difficult now. I don't know, I feel torn. First Kathmandu, then here, Bakslimaya – there is so much trouble there. And you too."

"Is it bad for me to be here now?" I smiled a bit wryly to myself.

"No, I didn't mean that. I can't let myself go, though. It's as if I were standing on a diving board and I cannot dive. You know, I often plunge into things without thought, just wildly. This time with you, I can't." Svein continued after a silence. "I've said before that Bakslimaya is my wife. I meant that in the full sense of the word. She has been sleeping with me." He spoke too delicately. I couldn't look at him then, wanting to be ashamed but not succeeding. I couldn't lie to him now nor negate what had gone before.

"What will happen to her when you leave?" I ought to hate him now, or at least feel jealous. I'm crazy.

"That's just it. I didn't think about the future when it started. I live so much in the moment and it was beautiful. We were drunk one night and we ended up in bed together. It just went on and on – she was my wife and I was a Nepali. But now, going back to Kathmandu, I realize I have only six months left. I don't know if I want to leave Nepal. I think I do. But I'm afraid of what will happen to her if I leave."

"It would ruin her life, wouldn't it?" I asked softly. "She has no one else. And no chance of employment." He started to speak as Ernie and Sarah laughed their way in the door, followed closely by Judy.

* * * * *

"What is your name?" The voice belonged to a boy. In America he'd have been about eight years old; here he was more likely fifteen or sixteen, I thought.

"Jessie."

"What is the name of your country?" The English was faultless.

"America."

"Why have you come to my village?"

"Just to visit," I answered, a bit astonished by the impeccable English. "And I wanted to see Nepal from the inside." The boy was probably Tibetan; though I couldn't tell for sure from the rags he wore. He carried himself with surprising dignity for such a little person. His eyes were a sharp rich brown. His questions continued with few errors and with good pronunciation. His aloofness slipped away as I talked and smiled at him, but he remained in command of the conversation.

"I hope you do not annoy with so many questions I ask you. I know little of life where you come."

"I enjoy it. You speak English quite well."

"I thank you. I do many wrongs. This is great pleasure to talking of a fine lady. You have a good face to look on."

"Thank you." So he had already learned the art of flattery.

But he was embarrassed now. "I do not know... my purpose is to glad you ... no" he corrected himself, "to gladden you. Is this correct?"

"It is correct. You have gladdened me." I smiled again.

"I must go now. School will begin."

"You must be a good student."

"Yes," he said thoughtfully, "I am the best student." No false modesty there, I thought. "I hope you see me again."

I spoke of the boy to Judy at supper.

"That must have been Karan. He speaks better English than anyone in the village. He's an orphan, I believe. His mother was Tibetan and his father is either dead or unknown. He's got a brother here also."

"Have you taught him so well?"

"Heavens no, I take no credit for Karan. He's a genius. He studies like a fiend and I help him and lend him books when I can. He has a rough life here; no friends at all in the school, I suppose because he is Tibetan. Kids used to pick on him but they've let up – he's fierce. They just ignore him now. We're probably the first friends he's ever had. He spends most of his time at Svein's now. I think he has visions of marrying Rukmini."

"How old is he?"

"Twelve."

"You're kidding!"

"No, I'm not. Rukmini has already had good offers. She's fifteen. And they're great friends."

A day or two later I saw him and his brother at Svein's house. It was the first time I had ever seen young people in a village talking freely without a chaperone. The three of them burst into gales of laughter from time to time, and Rukmini fell back on the mattress, rolling her eyes. Karan's brother was smaller and much more shy; Karan's aggressiveness had probably been acquired in the defense of them both. Karan greeted me at once and drew me into a careful conversation. He was refreshingly greedy for new words and information.

* * * * *

There was hardly an edge of moon showing when Judy and I left the house, stumbling over the large cobbles; a few oil lamps outlined the whitewashed houses on the street; several people moved about, some talking loudly, and others hurrying along close to the walls. We made our way through a maze of infinitesimal streets and alleys.

The temple courtyard was filling with people as we reached it. Immediately we entered the tiny temple, removing our sandals at the door. The floor was earthen without even cow dung to harden it, and a battered brass statue of Ganesha stood on the far wall. A few women greeted us. They were preparing leaf baskets of pooja, quite a lavish array of sweets, fruits, rice cakes, ghee, curd and flowers. The image soon disappeared behind the pile of offerings.

"This is the Festival of the 100,000 lights," whispered Judy. "One family has prepared all of the wicks by hand." People crowded in and we moved outside.

"For a while I was worried that I would offend people attending religious ceremonies. But they have always been pleased when I come, and often people send me darshan. This is partly why I've survived here as well as I have. I find it exceptionally beautiful. There's so little tradition in our society, I lap it up here like a thirsty cat. It's irrelevant that I don't believe in God. Do you know what I mean?"

The crowd of people surged clockwise around the temple in the dim light, moving in a slow wave. "Ten times around," whispered Judy before we were separated. I was carried along, just another body in a movement of bodies, engrossed in the experience. A few glanced curiously at me. We all stumbled together over the exposed roots of a Nim tree on the far side of the temple, staring into the path of light the moon gave, most of it caught miserly by the trees. There were people everywhere now, talking, silent, jostling and pushing. The movement was hypnotic, one step after another until one ceased to be the author of one's own motions but was part of a greater anonymous force commanding life for a space of time.

A hand gripped my wrist, a cold sweaty grip. The girl's teeth glowed in a recognizable smile. She was Sita's daughter. I followed her and found Judy already seated on a mat. I sat down, wordless. Someone handed me a stick that I guessed to be a kind of wand.

Small children played swords with their wands on the dirt, flourishing them like kukris and sticking them into one another's bellies. Latecomers moved around the temple while piles of wicks were prepared, soaking with ghee.

Flames licked up from the wicks, burning and writhing like a pile of hellish snakes. Sweet sticky smoke hung in the air. Children shoved their way closest to the fires, stirring their wands excitedly among the wicks, flicking them into the air. "It's for good fortune in the next year. You're to hope as hard as you can for the things you want." I waved my stick in the smoldering wicks, trying not to breathe in the smoke too deeply. Fifty more sticks knocked mine about like a boat in a storm, all poking for a prize place. Faces reddened, some knotted in concentration, others gentled in laughter.

Crowds of people were transformed into silhouettes edged in orange as the flames dimmed. The air dripped with the sticky smoke, and the sky turned an oppressive brown. We tried to enter the temple once again, but it was as full as it could be. Someone handed me darshan, a single lotus blossom; we found our sandals quickly and left.

Outside the temple walls I felt the breeze touch my wet cheeks. I was unaware I had been crying. The blossom was fresh in my palm.

* * * * *

The kitchen was lighted with a kerosene lamp and two candles. Bakslimaya tended the fire in the corner while we sat around on stools, half drunk and rocking with laughter.

"It was quite an ordeal," said Ernie. "I took Jessie around to the family I've done the most work with and they gave us the full treatment. You were damned lucky, you know. There were only four households."

"You wouldn't have believed it," I said. "Well, maybe you've been through it. It was lovely at first; going into the house, playing with the children and talking with the people. We were given mats to sit on and served a thumba of jherd. That's nearly a quart, you know, and as strong as beer. I was pleasantly stuffed when we left the first house, and I'd learned quite a lot from them. But three more! The only thing that differed in the next three houses was the way they prepared the egg they served with the jherd; in one it was boiled, in one fried, and in another curried. I staggered out of the next house, rolled out the third and crawled out the last. It was a nightmare. I had to finish the jherd; Ernie kept pressing on me how I'd insult them if I didn't, and how it would be a prime insult to skip one of the households. Good Lord, how do you ever study them if they're that hospitable?"

"You don't know Ernie. He can hold down gallons."

"I was sicker than I've ever been when we finished, but Ernie could still walk a straight line, almost."

"One thing I'll say, if they were competitive within the family I'd be dead or alcoholic by now. At least they all served the same amounts."

Sarah spoke up. "If you thought that was bad, you should have been here during Tihar. It beats Thanksgiving all to hell."

"It was beautiful, but sad too," broke in Judy. "People who eat only one or two manas of rice a week and meat probably eight or nine times a year served us incredible feasts. At one house we were given five different curries, all with meat. That family I know well; the children are always hungry, they have only one small pot of rice each day. They gave us so much that we were all sick together afterwards. You feel terribly guilty, but it would be far more cruel to refuse."

The gaiety increased in direct proportion to the amount of roxi consumed. Bakslimaya kept the cups filled. She was drinking too at Ernie's invitation. A large bowl of roasted maize and lentils stood before us. Ernie boomed out a song. He had a raucous voice, but Judy and Sarah saved it from total ruin with strong sopranos. They enjoyed themselves; making a lot of noise was not something they permitted themselves often.

Svein sat quietly by, a bit out of it, listening to the night sounds and sipping the strong liquor. His face had settled into an oddly serious expression in the past couple of days; spontaneity had left him for the moment. I got up and went to him. Bakslimaya followed my movements with her eyes. I touched him lightly on the shoulder.

Fast as fury Bakslimaya was across the room, and before I saw her move, her hand came down like a whiplash. I thought at first she had hit me, then, raped by hideous pain as she yanked the knife out, I screamed. My breath was tied in knots. "What the fuck..." Ernie grabbed Bakslimaya's wrist and the knife dropped to the floor. She twisted out of his grasp and ran from the house. No one followed.

I slipped to my knees. I detached myself from the pain as easily as a lizard discards his tail, exhausted from that instant of consciousness, more intense than a human can bear. Already half-frozen, I hung onto my left shoulder and watched the blood coming between my fingers and dripping on the floor in a steady flow. I watched with glassy interest.

"Someone do something!" screamed Sarah. "She's dying!" Dying... who? Oh no, NO. I closed my eyes as a frantic anguish gripped me. It can't all end here now, not now.

"Don't be a fool!" snapped Judy. "Have you a medical kit?"

"No."

"Nothing at all?" asked Judy with irritation.

"No, I'm sorry."

"Rip up a sheet then and bring me the rest of the roxi." She'd taken over. I relaxed then, deciding to let life take care of itself. I lay in a kind of trance, cold and aware. "And then figure out something we can use for a stretcher."

"You're going to move her?" Svein spoke drunkenly.

"We can't leave her here, can we? So Bakslimaya can do a better job next time? And I'll probably have to sew it."

They laid me on a mattress and Judy cut away the kurta.

"Jessie, this is going to hurt like crazy. I'm sorry but we've got to do it. You can scream all you want, we don't mind."

She poured on the alcohol. But it didn't hurt, just stung a little. My shoulder was still there. I tried to smile but my teeth were chattering too hard. They covered me with a blanket.

"How bad is it?" My first words were clumsy. Judy was distant.

"You're not going to die at any rate. But it's going to take more than a Band-Aid to fix you up. Do you think you have enough strength to be moved? We can carry you."

"Yes," I whispered. "Please."

Ernie came in. "We've got a bamboo ladder that will do."

"Good, I'm glad there's someone around here who can keep his head. Everyone else seems to fly off the handle one way or another." Then, "But not a word from your cynical side or you'll have *me* up in hysterics."

They carried me down slowly. I was aware of the cool night and the strong moonlight in my face. People called out from their houses. The stretcher rocked like a boat in a storm. I felt ill. The wound throbbed now, pounding the pain through my entire body. An eternity later we reached the house.

The operation took about an hour and a half, Judy working gingerly but determinedly. I remember nothing but the faces; Sita in the doorway, her daughters awe-stricken with huge round eyes, Svein in a corner not looking at me, Sarah cowering, and Ernie holding my hand with concern and interest in his face. He made light comments from time to time to relieve Judy's tension. His hand kept me there.

Judy looked up, exhausted. "Clear out, everyone. Please. We'll worry about everything else in the morning."

I wanted nothing more from the world than sleep.

* * * * *

I awoke to the throbbing of my shoulder; I must have started to roll over on it. A thin line of brightness ran where the shutters met; it was dark outside. Weakness washed through my body as I tried to sit up. Damn.

Sunlight carried the freshness of the mountains into the room. Sita appeared in the doorway. She made the sign of eating with her hand and looked quite pleased when I nodded yes. I ate a bit.

My first visitor was Karan. He came bearing a handful of

wildflowers, and paused outside the door.

"Jessie-sister?"

"Yes."

"May I have the honor to come inside your room?"

"Of course, Karan."

"I have heard of your sad accident. I came to tell you how I am troubled."

"Thank you."

"You have pain?"

"Sometimes." He looked around the room curiously as he spoke, taking in every detail.

"You fight with Bakslimaya, isn't it?"

"Is that what people are saying?"

He considered this. "People in this village say you want also of being wife to Svein-sir. Is it true?"

"I don't know Karan."

He persisted. "But you want of being wife to Svein-sir?"

I was silent a few moments. "No."

It was a restless day. I was a flickering candle. People came in and out all day and I slept in between, waking heavily as one does during day sleeping. Conversations hovered over my head. Now and then I would reach out and grab a word or phrase. There was talk of a helicopter and a telegram. I knew that I had a fever; sometimes the sweat rolled down my forehead as if I were reliving that first day's climb from the terrai.

Late the following afternoon Svein made his appearance. By some chance they were all there; the day's work was done.

It was still a solemn Svein; he had grown accustomed to his thoughts. I was happy to see him and told him so, but I thought ruefully I wished it wasn't so. He sat down on one of the bright Tibetan carpets, his forehead wrinkled in contemplation.

"Any word from Bakslimaya?" asked Ernie.

"She came back last night." He sat awhile. The others waited patiently for him to find the words. They knew him well enough to know when to give him time. He started slowly. "You know about my relationship with her. She is like my wife. I have made love to her."

"Svein," I broke in, "if you're worried about whether I'm going to have her arrested – I wouldn't even know how, let alone want to. I'm not angry or revengeful, really, I'm not; I just don't understand."

"But she tried to murder you!" cried Sarah with a note of outrage. "She might be dangerous."

"Shut up, Sarah," said Ernie disgustedly. "We all know she isn't insane. She must have had a reason for it."

"Yes." Svein hesitated. "She's pregnant."

"Christ almighty!" exclaimed Ernie.

"Oh Svein," said Judy simultaneously. I kept quiet.

"Are you sure?"

"Why shouldn't I be? She's never lied to me."

"It could be a trick."

He shook his head wearily. "No. It's no use trying to eradicate the fact. It's there. I just don't know what to do."

"Svein," put in Sarah, "you're always jumping into things

without thought for the consequences. And for once..."

"Hold on, Sarah. Svein needs help, not criticism."

"Well, he should have thought about that before he started screwing around with her. And I don't see how we can help. He's got to get himself out of the mess."

"Sarah," said Judy, "I think he just needs to talk to us. He doesn't expect us to solve his problems."

But Sarah was on her way, this time to defend Bakslimaya. It would never have occurred to her that she was being inconsistent. "Whose shoulder is Bakslimaya going to cry on? She's the one who's going to suffer. Her life is wrecked; what do you suppose her position in this village will be now? And how do you suppose she's going to earn enough money to feed herself? Why don't we think about her?"

"We are thinking about her."

"Bullshit." Her voice lacked conviction.

"They both walked into this with open eyes."

"Are you kidding? With lovely pink elephants in front of them."

Svein laughed. "It is true Sarah. But I love her."

"Do you?" asked Sarah, somewhat mollified. "Do you know what love is?"

"Let's not get into a philosophical discussion," said Judy.

"How can I say what love is? Perhaps I don't know at all. What do you think I should do, Sarah; marry her?"

"I don't know. At least you could send her money – honestly, I doubt she can support herself once you leave. No one will hire her as a cook. No one needs a cook."

"She got along before you came," said Ernie.

"Yeah, but all of us spoil the people who work for us," answered Judy. "We raise their standard of living quite a bit, and their social standing. And then when we leave, the whole thing deflates like a balloon. It's cruel. Svein's not the only one; we're all in the same boat."

"How do you feel about marrying her?" asked Sarah.

"In a sense we are married. In terms of this culture we're married. She's been talking about coming back with me to Norway for the past weeks. I've never encouraged her. I just don't know."

"Man, you're crazy." Ernie spoke vehemently. "Bakslimaya would be miserable there. I bet she hasn't the remotest idea of distances or anything. She's never even seen a car, let alone a city or paved street, or electric light. You might be able to swing it with a young girl, but Bakslimaya's too old."

"She's not old."

"She's got to be at least thirty with a fifteen year old daughter. I bet you ten dollars she's over thirty-five. Seriously now, can you imagine her in downtown Oslo, shopping; in western clothes? It doesn't work."

"I can imagine Rukmini there. I don't know, maybe that's too easy an excuse. For leaving her, I mean. I'm arrogant enough to think that I could keep her happy."

"You're the best thing that ever happened to her. I don't mean to sound cynical, it's true. She ran away from her first husband, the villagers say. He must have been horrid. You don't beat her, you listen to her, you're kind, you bring her gifts, you earn plenty of money and you share it with her. No wonder she's in love with you. Listen, I think there's racism in all of us, or prejudice, call it what you will. It may be suppressed, but you've got it. How are you going to feel introducing her to your friends? She's had no education at all. She'll probably never learn to speak English well. She's not even beautiful; she's a middle-aged woman. She won't even be able to cook for you. Do you think you're going to want rice and vegetables back in Norway? You'll be ashamed of her and she'll be lonely as hell."

"What about staying here?" asked Judy.

"That would be the best solution for Bakslimaya, of course. I've considered it. I don't know. I like Nepal. When I started, I just dived in without thought of leaving. But I never thought of spending my whole life here. That's where my selfishness comes in. I don't know if I'd be happy here. I don't want to be tied down yet... Jessie, you haven't said a word. Will you say something?"

I looked up, strained by the question. "I have no wisdom to offer. All I can say is that no matter what decision you make or how you make it, you are both going to suffer. There's no way we can alleviate that suffering; we'll just be with you in any way we can be."

"Thanks." He sounded as if he wanted me to say more.

"One more thing," I said. "Why did she attack me? Did she see us that afternoon?"

"Yes, she did. But it wasn't only that. I stopped sleeping with her after I returned from Kathmandu. I thought the whole thing was becoming too serious, and it would hurt her less to end it now rather than later." Svein looked at me, straight and hard, and I knew from his eyes he had done it for me. At the pit of my stomach I felt a ball of exultation, then guilt; what a bitch I am.

"Can you tell her she has nothing to fear from me?"

He nodded.

"Svein," I whispered before he left, "I wish I could help you. But I know if I ever see you again you'll be past the decision and past any need of me."

"That's when I'll come," he answered, and bent his way out into the night.

* * * *

Ernie walked as quietly as he could up the wooden stairs to my room, but I heard the gentle swish of his boots. It was a moonless night, depressingly dark, and he carried a flashlight he did not use. He knocked softly on the door.

"It's me, Ernie. Are you awake?"

"Come in." I lit a candle, delighted to be visited this particular midnight, and greeted him cheerfully. "I can't sleep. I'm just lying here feeling sorry for myself. I guess I've been sleeping altogether too much these past couple of days."

He nodded. "I figured this would be the last chance to see you alone. If the telegrams make it, the helicopter will come tomorrow."

"That will cost a mint, won't it?" The fact was beginning to penetrate.

"Not so awfully much if it drops you on the terrai. You can get a regular plane from there." He paused. "I'm really sorry this happened to you."

"So am I."

I looked at Ernie sitting there cross-legged, his hands dangling on his knees. In the candlelight he looked even more like a pirate. He launched into his tale, speaking laconically, and I watched him as he spoke. He was telling about a quarrel. I guessed that more than any one of them, Ernie understood Nepal. His relationships were much the same there as they would be in any part of the world. He drank and quarreled and laughed; he liked some people and disliked others and was frank about it. He observed their way of life without detachment just as a man will examine the life of a good friend, not passing judgments or evaluations but simply with an interest and appreciation. People knew him for a fellow human. And those who liked him, liked him well for he gave back in good measure what he received.

Ernie was speaking of Karan. He had borrowed a dictionary several months before, and neither returned it nor mentioned it. "I asked him about it a couple of times. Then I ran into him up there at Svein's, he's courtin' Rukmini, you know. I was a bit drunk and irritated – I meant it half in jest but it was serious too if you know what I mean – I said, 'You little bugger, you mean to steal it.' I should have laughed it off or something, but I was mad, and his face went all red as if he was trying not to cry and he stomped out. Later I felt guilty, but I was still mad at him. It really must have been a blow to his pride. And Rukmini saw it all too. I just didn't think. And then passing where he and his brother live, he came out and wanted to fight, to defend his honor, you know. That got me where it hurts – why I could kill the little bastard in two seconds if I wanted to. Of course I refused. I just walked away, but I probably insulted him even more by doing that.

"Well, a couple of days later I received the book and a letter with it, the prettiest letter you ever saw. I doubt an American could do as well. I know I couldn't. There wasn't a mistake in it and it was hand written better than anything I've ever seen here. He told me politely I'd insulted him deeply and that he hoped I would never speak to him again. I can't remember the words; it was a real masterpiece, that letter, I still have it. It shamed me. Think what it must have cost him – we're the first friends he's ever had. I wrote back asking him to forgive me. I really did. He wrote me a fancy reply saying he would forgive me. It must have been hard for him to do that. But we're still not friends. There's a strain every time we meet up.

"I want to send him to school, that boarding school in Kathmandu. It doesn't cost an awful lot and I could keep him there several years without it hurting. I don't want him to know I'm doing it; it might hurt his pride. He's smart. He hasn't a chance of getting anywhere here. I hope someone else will send his brother next year when he completes his exams. If they don't, I will, they're always talking about it, but you know how far that goes. What really matters is that somebody somewhere gives a damn."

I nodded, thinking about how lives are interwoven. "I'll take him with me."

Ernie held my hand a few moments. "Okay, see you in the morning."

* * * * *

I lay watching morning hit the mountain, transforming the colors of the layered fields and the whitewashed huts. I had set aside the concept of time and now it was confronting me like a thick stonewall. This afternoon I would be back in Kathmandu, back inside the mad rhythm of a city day and in a hospital. There was no desire in me to leave the village. I thought how easily I could stay a month or a year, how intense life was here. It was a shade of living I had missed without knowing it, an awareness of detail that had dulled in natural defense against ugliness. My eyes were open; the simple experience of walking down the narrow streets was enough to fill a day. I felt more welcome here than I had felt elsewhere, yet I was a stranger. Sitting on a mat and drinking tea there was no awkwardness for me, not even in the absence of spoken language; there was the language of touch, expression, and intuition, and it was somehow more honest than the other. I had the feeling that the people I came to know, knew me well.

What would I remember later; the quality of the experience, my agonizing over Svein, the stabbing... would it leave a scar? Tension lived with the sahibs, not even Svein, so hang-loose, escaped that. I knew that given a choice I would rather be alone in a village so as not to be torn both ways except inside myself. I had once been lonely enough to know that there is a humanness common to all, a humanity in any other being that can assuage the emptiness. The loneliness one lives from smile to smile, feasting on a few words.

I wondered if Svein would come, thinking about how odd it was that I attached little emotion to the event. If he didn't come, I would feel no resentment; I had never believed in good-byes. Others would stand there crying, but I often laughed for I could not feel the abruptness of parting. For me it occurred gradually and gently; I kept the reality of people with me a long time, until they faded in the throes of a new experience.

A leaf-bud. The word slipped into my consciousness. I played with it a moment. Svein was a bud, light green and exquisite. I longed to spread him apart with my fingers, but I knew it was too soon. The bud would shrivel, turn brown and fall. I should be able to love Svein without wanting him, like loving a flower too well to want to pluck it.

I heard his steps on the stairs and there he was in the doorway grinning. Maybe he doesn't believe in good-byes either, I thought with relief. We sat together in the soft early minutes before the sun is really born.

Before we left, I ducked into the kitchen and gave Sita a few rupees I had, a small sum of money even in the mountains. I wanted to give something. Sita was enormously pleased. She stroked my cheek, accepting the gift for what it was, not payment or alms. Her pleasure was so great I told Judy about it. "Tell your scoundrel she's been wonderful to me the entire time."

Judy laughed. "A couple of months ago a nurse visited here, stayed with me and gave Sita 15 rupees when she left. Sita spit in her face."

Villagers were gathering in the open space near the schoolhouse that served as a market place on Sundays. The place was swarming with people; helicopters were a great attraction. Svein and I stood above them on the footpath. I looked at the village and the hills beyond it and the highest places on earth beyond them, wanting to be drunk with my perception, letting the beauty flow with all the emotions I was experiencing. Svein appeared almost happy, his hair reflecting the sunrays. He stood astride with his thumbs hooked through the shoulder straps of the pack he was carrying for me. He was strong on that hill, and straight, and tall.

"I'm glad I've known you." I said it without thinking.

"I'm glad I've loved you." It was a half-mockery of words, but it was the only way he could have said it. We laughed at ourselves, and each other, close in those last light moments. I left him then, smiling so hard it hurt.

.. V ..

I walked in the narrow cobbled streets of Patan, bittersweet in the transition from mountain to city. It was still Nepal, yet it wasn't: jeeps, trucks, and bicycles rushed past, mangy dogs roamed the temples for edible offerings, and the gutters were filthy. I could understand why the village people had said to me, "Kathmandu? But that isn't Nepal, it's another country." To many it was a legendary city, the very end of the world where the streets were paved with gold, where things were fabulously inexpensive, where one could hear music from a mechanical box, where the king lived in a palace too luxurious for description. A stranger might have found it a wild potpourri of religions: temples for an array of gods that would have taxed the wildest imagination, temples built with turned-up roofs like smiles piled on top of one another, sculptures in every imaginable pose from the Kama Sutra, gold-covered Buddhas in blissful serenity, carved animals that the world might never have seen the like of otherwise.

Someone from USAID drove by in a Mercedes-Benz, honking in the slow-moving street. A child clutched at my sari, terrified at the sunlight glancing off the shiny metal. To the amazement of several bystanders, I picked up the child and held her close a few moments. Suddenly I heard a flurry of motion behind me. Turning, I faced an extraordinary couple running to me, both haloed in white hair. The man wore floppy trousers and carried a cane over his arm as if waiting for the day that he might actually use it. He sported a handlebar mustache that bounced up and down with the rhythm of his trot. His wife hung on for dear life, laughing in delight, her flowered dress looking not at all out of place in the odd city.

They parked themselves in front of me. "Do you know where we can get some hash, huh, huh?" I stared at them in astonishment. Their eyes sparkled with the eagerness of young children.

The woman laughed. "We promised our grandson we'd try it, and he said anyone would know where to get it."

Her husband added soberly, "We understand it's legal here." He was full of suppressed excitement, like sneaking downstairs at Christmas before you're supposed to, I thought.

I reached into my pocket to the hard lump Judy had placed there before the helicopter took off. I handed it to them. "Just take this. I won't be needing it."

"Oh, thank you!" exclaimed the woman. Her husband nodded.

"How do we use it?" he asked.

"Do you smoke a pipe?"

"Yes."

"Just crumble some and mix it with your tobacco."

"Thank you ever so much. You're quite sure you won't be needing it?"

"Quite sure," I answered as they rushed off. Crazy world.

Afterword

Cultural Exploration and the Quest for Authentic Connection

One Way Ticket is a quiet, reflective, even philosophical story that captures an aspect of the 1960s central to the expansion of consciousness in both an outward and inward sense that was characteristic of the time. During the 60s, a generational cohort of North American and European youth emerged from the consumer society in search of both a personal identity and a way of life that was more authentic than the one they were being offered. For some, this quest was highly spiritual; for some, it was service oriented – doing good work in the world, especially helping those struggling in circumstances of poverty, racism, and lack of resources. For some young people, the search involved both dimensions – personal growth in identity, and ethical growth in compassion, service, and cross-cultural understanding. Young people began to travel in increasing numbers to cultures other than their own with this mix of orientations.

U.S. President John Kennedy established the Peace Corp in 1961, which became a leading edge of cross-cultural experience for young Americans. A new form of popular anthropological literature was emerging that served to open windows into cultural worlds beyond those of North America and Europe. These included now classic works such as *Return to Laughter* by Elenore Smith Bowen (pen name of Laura Bohannan), *Stranger and Friend* by Hortense Powdermaker, *The Harmless People* by Elizabeth Marshall Thomas, *Freedom and Culture* by Dorothy Lee, *Four Ways of Being Human* by Gene Lisitzky, *Coming of Age in Samoa* by Margaret Mead, and *Patterns of Culture* by Ruth Benedict. Marshall McLuhan coined the term "global village" during this period to describe the coming cultural effect of worldwide electronic communication. There was a growing realization that various social, economic, and ecological problems were now global in scope and a new worldwide perspective and understanding was needed. The worldviews of Asian cultural traditions were making steady inroads into Western philosophical thought and spiritual practice. The wisdom of indigenous peoples worldwide was increasingly evident as the integrity and viability of industrial-consumer civilization became increasingly doubtful. This amalgamation of cultural ferment and this quest for alternative realities became central to the ethos of the 60s.

One Way Ticket deftly illuminates this ethos of the era. It is like a miniature in which a larger reality can be glimpsed. It is like a shooting star that leaves an indelible trace across the firmament of memory for those of us who shared the quest of those years. For those in subsequent generations who recognize the significance and value of this quest, it is perhaps a cautionary tale as well. *One Way Ticket*, while a slim volume, provides penetrating insight into both the positive dynamics and the hazardous circumstances of cross-cultural experience. Students of cultural exploration, like Sanno Keeler, who have investigated various alternative realities, and have recorded the trajectories of their experience, can be helpful guides for those who continue to seek horizons of learning that lead to engagement with human solidarity. Sanno Keeler died in 1991 but she left us this luminous story from her cross-cultural experience and her quest for authentic connection.

Keith Helmuth
March 2015

Sanno Keeler and Jim Spickard hiking in Norway, 1980

Remembering Sanno Keeler

I heard about Friends World College from Sanno Keeler on our first date. We had met each other a few weeks before at a contra dance festival. We seemed to be the only two dancers with a social conscience, so she invited me for a day of canoeing on Elkhorn Slough, on the central California coast. I arrived, we talked and canoed for six or seven hours, and I heard about her childhood, her parent's early deaths, Quaker boarding school in backwoods British Columbia, and her travels in the FWC program. I was fascinated. I had been abroad, of course; in fact, I almost didn't return to the U.S. in the late 1960s, the political situation being what it was. Yet Sanno had such a bright outlook on the world. She had an affirming sense of human possibility, a get-in-there-and-fix-things attitude that I couldn't help but find attractive. Day stretched into evening, we went back to her house and cooked a small diner, and I essentially never left. Ten years, two kids, and a lot of memories later, she died at home of breast cancer, surrounded by family and friends. I think she had been happy. I know I was – and I was extremely lucky that she was a part of my life.

Sanno had lots of stories about FWC. She was in the first class, so the school was just a few steps ahead of her as she moved through its foreign programs. Her second year, in Tromse, Norway, was especially formative. Her host had actively resisted the German invasion in World War Two, which meshed with her politics and her memory of her activist father. I think it also gave her a stable family life, something every orphan needs. We visited them in Norway the first summer we were together. Køre (the father) took us to my own great-grandfather's village, near where he had been raised. We bicycled up the Gudbrands Valley and across the Jotenheimen Mountains, staying with people she had known. I was impressed with how easily she picked up again with folks she had not seen in years. She had the facility for deep friendships.

I heard fewer stories about Tanzania and India. She talked of working with Jane Goodall, and the perspective that watching chimpanzees gave her on our own babies. ("Look," she'd say, "It's an 'excited food grunt'.") Of India, I learned about Vinoba Bhave, the various Gandhian movements, and the complexity of Indian life. Our daughter, Janaki, is named after one of her FWC teachers. I sensed there were a few scars from those years, but she never talked about them.

Nor did I learn until recently about *One Way Ticket*. I knew Sanno had written stories in school and I had read some of them, but she didn't share this one. She didn't write much during our first years together, either. She enjoyed her job teaching migrant farmworker kids and was delighted when we had two of our own. She took up writing again in the late 1980s. She crafted several stories and a few novellas, one of which she worked on during her last illness. I suspect she would have pursued a career at it, had she lived. I sensed something stirring in her. I periodically wonder what path she would have taken, and how it would have affected the rest of us. I'll never know.

I do know, though, that she was a deep spirit. Our family is glad to have *One Way Ticket* published and to share it with the Friends World community. Its themes of cross-cultural understanding and social justice were at the heart of Sanno's life. Friends World College was, too.

Jim Spickard
March 2015

About Friends World College

In the early 1960s, members of New York Yearly Meeting of the Religious Society of Friends (Quakers), led by Dr. George Nicklin, began working toward the establishment of Friends World College (FWC). In 1963, a summer institute was conducted under the direction of Harold Taylor at Jericho, Long Island, New York to test the concept of a higher education program based on multi-cultural participation in a world education program. Friends World Institute was established as a four-year liberal arts program in 1965. Its campus was the compound of buildings that had been the U.S. Air Force officers' quarters at Mitchel Field, Westbury, Long Island, New York. The Institute received its charter as a College from the New York State Board of Regents in 1968.

The original Committee on a Friends World College had envisioned a multi-cultural residential program in the New York City area, which, in its global perspective, would develop a close association with the United Nations.

When Morris Mitchell was hired to establish Friends World College on a full-time basis, he brought with him a vision and design for a world education program that dramatically altered the development of the College.* He proposed, and the Board of Trustees approved, the establishment of study centers in each of the world's major cultural regions to which students would travel, and, in the course of four years, come to acquire a truly global education; an education *in* the real world of human cultural diversity and *about* the problems of security and wellbeing with which all societies must cope. The design of the College became peripatetic and the curriculum oriented toward what Morris Mitchell called "world problems and their emerging solutions." As successive groups of students were admitted, study centers were opened in Latin America, Europe, East Africa, India, and Japan. In later years programs were also based in the Middle East and China.

In the early 1970s, the College's North American campus and world headquarters moved to the Livingston Estate at Lloyd Harbor, Long Island. FWC continued to operate as an independent liberal arts college until 1991, when it became the Friends World Program of Long Island University. Long Island University maintained and developed FWC's unique

---

* *See* Morris Mitchell, 1967. *World Education: Revolutionary Concept*. New York: Pageant Press.

See also Keith Helmuth, 2015. "The Evolution of Environmental Education: Morris Mitchell and the Early Years of Friends World College, 1965–1970" in *Tracking Down Ecological Guidance*, Woodstock NB: Chapel Street Editions.

design and world education program. In 2013 the Program was renamed Global College of Long Island University and is now referred to as LIU Global. (see http://liu.edu/Global). Over all these years the program has remained much the same as was originally established and developed during the early years of Friends World College, and the Quaker origin is still referenced in the history of LIU Global. Students study, work, live, and travel worldwide, designing and carrying out projects, making connections, and establishing relationships that add up to the unique experience of a global education in the real world.

Keith Helmuth
March 2015

About Friends World College
Memories Project

The publication of *One Way Ticket* marks the launch of the Friends World College Memories Project. This Project has developed from reunions of Friends World College students in 2008 and 2014, and from the 50th Anniversary Celebration held at Long Island University in 2015.

The FWC Memories Project aims to:

- provide a forum for the sharing of writings, photos, journals, and other archive materials from students, staff, and supporters of the College;
- establish a dedicated space to bring together and share the archival materials via publications (including ebooks), the establishment of a website, and other processes for guarding, as well as celebrating, the history and development of FWC;

- protect, celebrate, and learn from the development, history, and experiences of Friends World College.

There is a lot of important and rich archival information about the early vision of New York Yearly Meeting Quakers who founded the College, the tasks of achieving the opening of the program, the students, staff, and other supporters of Friends World College. The multiple achievements of all those involved in making FWC a reality, and the lessons learned along the way need to be brought together for sharing.

I came from away from the 2008 reunion fascinated and excited by the multiple stories I heard of our experiences, our "life journeys" and the impact FWC had on each of us. We were in essence the "guinea pigs" or pioneers for this global, experiential, education experiment. My fascination and excitement has grown into a strong desire to find a way to tell some of these stories of our life journeys and explore the impact of Friends World on us as individuals, including the educational impact of this unique experience.

Over the past year I have dedicated time to going through some archives from the early years. There are some major collections at the Friends Historical Library (Swarthmore College). LIU Global is the caretaker of a lot of other materials, including student journals and theses. Under the auspices of LIU Global, I had the opportunity to organize and appropriately archive the student journals I found from the first eight entering classes (September 1965 – January 1969). It was amongst these boxes that I found Sanno's Keeler's novella. Once I started reading it, I couldn't put it down.

It feels that now is the appropriate time to begin to compile and explore the student journal archives, find more hidden treasures, learn about experiential and global education from our recorded experiences, and share this material – not only amongst the FWC / LIU Global community but to a wider audience who recognize the importance of this model of education as a focus for addressing ongoing global issues. It is time to tell our stories, share them widely and assess the real power and impact of global experiential education.

To date, we are not a formal association but a small group of people dedicated to ensuring that we appropriately preserve the stories and documentation, as well as learn from the archives to inform ongoing education endeavors. We are hoping the broad FWC community will contribute more archival materials and support the full launch of the Friends World College Memories Project.

Susie Daniel
March 2015

For further information, please contact
fwi.journeys@gmail.com

About the Editors

Susie Daniel was member of the 4th entering class of Friends World College, February 1967. Keith Helmuth was a member of the faculty of Friends World College, 1967-1970.